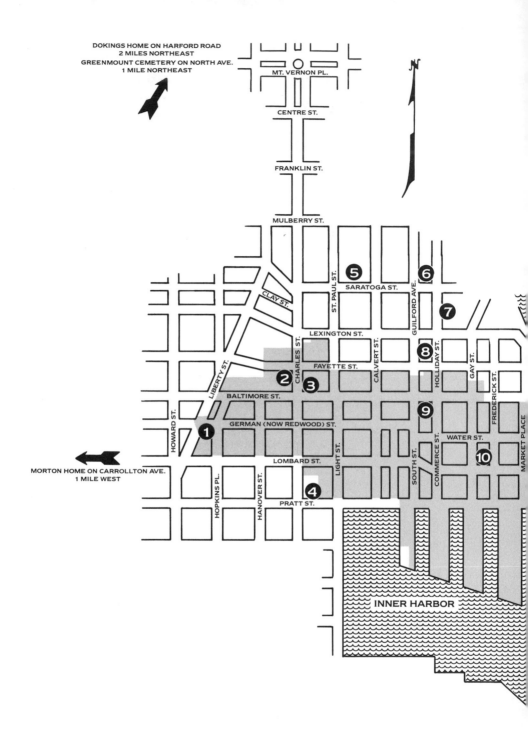

Landmarks of Big Fire in Baltimore

1. Hurst Building (where fire started)
2. Equitable Building
3. Morton Shoe Store
4. Anderson and Ireland Building
5. City (now Mercy) Hospital
6. House of Welsh
7. Peale Museum
8. City Hall
9. Sun Building
10. Morton Shoe Factory
11. Lombard Street Bridge
12. St. Leo's Church

Shaded areas were destroyed by the fire.

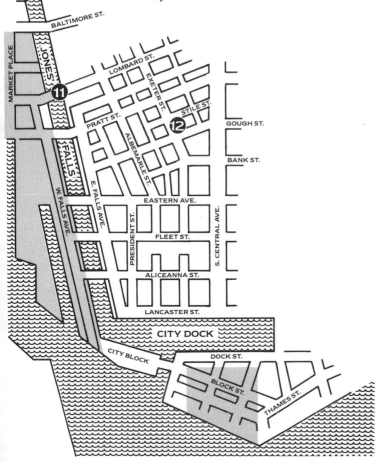

Big Fire in Baltimore

Rosa Kohler Eichelberger

BIG FIRE in BALTIMORE

illustrated by
Rex Schneider

Stemmer House
PUBLISHERS, INC.
Owings Mills, Maryland
1979

Inquiries should be directed to
STEMMER HOUSE PUBLISHERS, INC.
2627 CAVES ROAD
OWINGS MILLS, MARYLAND, 21117

Published simultaneously in Canada
by George J. McLeod, Limited, Don Mills, Ontario

A *Barbara Holdridge book*
Printed and bound in the United States of America
First Edition

Library of Congress Cataloging in Publication Data

Eichelberger, Rosa Kohler.
    Big fire in Baltimore.

    SUMMARY: The desire of a boy to become a
Western Union messenger is fulfilled during the
conflagration that destroyed much of Baltimore in
1904.
    1. Baltimore—Fire, 1904—Juvenile fiction.
[1. Baltimore—Fire, 1904—Fiction. 2. Fires—
Fiction] I. Schneider, Rex. II. Title.
PZ7.E338Bi   [Fic]   78-31311
ISBN 0-916144-36-4
ISBN 0-916144-37-2 pbk.

Preface

Big Fire in Baltimore is a story, and the characters in it are story people.

However, the Baltimore Fire of 1904 was very real. It was one of the greatest disasters ever to strike a major American city, and the worst ever suffered by Baltimore. More than 1500 buildings were destroyed, an area of almost 140 acres or about seventy city blocks was devastated, and the entire business district was wiped out.

In this book I have tried to recreate the locale—using the names of actual buildings, businesses (except for the fictional Morton Shoe Company) and streets—and the atmosphere of the catastrophe that affected the lives of thousands of people very much like those portrayed here.

R.K.E.

Big Fire in Baltimore

1

In the city of Baltimore, the winter day was coming to a close.

Tod Morton trudged up Carrollton Avenue toward home. Nothing had gone right today. His father was cross at him again, and again it was all because he wanted so much to become a telegraph operator and work for the Western Union.

He braced himself against the wind, and pulled his stocking cap down over his ears. For once the weather was so cold that his knitted gloves were on his hands instead of being stuffed into his pockets. His heavy overcoat came only to the bottom of his kneepants, and he wished he were wearing men's trousers. He would have to wait a while, however, for long pants, because he was only twelve years old and not very tall.

Lost in his gloomy thoughts, he kicked a stone off the sidewalk and saw it hit the lacy edges of ice in the gutter. He started across the street without noticing the trolley car that bounced toward him, but hurriedly jumped out of the way as the motorman kept stomping on the bell.

He passed "Miss Kate's" candy store, not far from his home, and saw himself in her big glass window. Seeing his drooping shoulders, he straightened up and knew he looked taller. He took off his cap, ran his fingers through his unruly blonde hair, and then once again pulled the cap down over his ears.

It wasn't fair, he thought, for his father to send him home from the store. But maybe he had been too "sassy." Maybe he should not have said what he did.

"I don't want to deliver shoes," he had declared. "I *hate* shoes! Now if I could deliver messages, Western Union messages—"

That was when his father had become furious and sent him home. This left the burden of all the Saturday night deliveries for their one delivery boy, Vincent deSales, otherwise known as 'Sales" because he was always trying to substitute for the salesmen and make a "sale" of shoes.

Tod grudgingly admitted now that his father had reason for his anger. The salesmen in the store had heard every word, and for him, the son of Todhunter Morton, to say he hated *shoes* was almost like saying he hated his *father*. Yet why couldn't his father understand that delivering shoes, even the Morton Shoe, was very different from delivering messages for the Western Union Telegraph Company?

There was not much left of Saturday afternoon, but he would still have a little time to practice his telegraphy, as he did each day. The gate latch had proved a perfect sending machine for the Morse alphabet, even though his messages went only into the wide open spaces of the nearby yards and alleys. Maybe this was a good thing, because he sometimes sent out strange messages. Sometimes it was fun to send out words like LAMK. He would always laugh to himself when he sent out this word, because it had puzzled everyone. At one time even the operators taking the messages did not know what it meant. Was it a new business using only its initials? Was it an organization? Or a political party? Everyone wondered. Then the simple truth came out.

A man wanted to send his wife love and kisses, but since the Western Union charged for telegrams by the word, he had used his own way to end his message in one word instead of four. He and his wife knew that LAMK stood for "LOVE AND MANY KISSES." When the story of this secret code had been revealed finally, even the Western Union operators had had a good laugh at their unsuccessful efforts to solve the mystery.

Tod knew there was something else he must do before he could practice his telegraphy, and that was to take his dog, Gerry, for a walk. Not that Gerry really needed to be *taken* anywhere, but Tod hoped that with enough walks, Gerry would be content to stay home the rest of the time. Perhaps if he went walking often enough, he would not wander off by himself, going where he pleased, and coming home when outdoor pleasures failed, or when he was hungry, or when he just felt like coming back.

For more than a year, Tod and his family had been trying to understand Gerry, ever since a man had given Tod not only the dog but also a dollar to take him away. The Mortons' hope now was that Gerry had finally reached his full growth, and would not get any bigger. At the time of Gerry's introduction to them he was already two feet high, and no one knew then that he was just a puppy. But now he was pony-size, with short hair that was black and white where it was not brown. Some unknown ancestor had given him a graceful feathery tail that curled over his back in a question mark. Mr. Morton always said that Gerry would never make "best of breeds" in a dog show, but he would surely take first prize for "all of breeds."

Nor had Gerry ever learned any tricks. After a few disastrous efforts to teach him, Tod had found it best to just forget about the whole thing. Gerry was smart enough, but he was just too big to do the usual tricks that small dogs could do. To sit up and beg was out of the question, for Gerry's huge body just collapsed on the floor, making a noise like a pile of shoe boxes tumbling down. When Tod finally persuaded Gerry to "speak," it sounded so much like thunder that the Mortons feared the neighbors might run to their windows to see if a storm was coming. If Gerry tried to roll over, everything rolled with him, chairs and rugs and even a table at one time. Finally Tod and his family settled for just Gerry, loving and loveable, without any tricks except those of his own invention.

One trick that Gerry had learned all by himself was to "purr." He purred for everything, to say "hello" or "thank you" or sometimes to chase away someone he didn't like. When he was happy the throaty rumble came out with a sound that strangers often mistook for a growl. When he was delighted the purr rose in a crescendo that became a roar.

Smiling to himself as he thought of Gerry, Tod began to hurry a little more. Then suddenly he stood stock-still.

A crowd of boys was walking down Carrollton Avenue. As they came closer, Tod began to recognize his own friends. They were hovering over something in their midst. Tod caught a flicker of black and white fur. It couldn't be Gerry! Gerry was in their backyard with the gate latched.

The boys were all ganged together, but peering through their legs, Tod became convinced that the creature with black and white fur and a hint of brown could only be Gerry! But how could he have gotten out of the yard?

"Here Gerry! Here Gerry!" he called.

Detaching himself from the group, Gerry came bounding down the street. Tod braced himself against the nearest steps—Gerry's enthusiasm could be overwhelming. The dog skidded to a stop, reared up and put his two front paws on Tod's shoulders, purring his welcome into Tod's ear.

"What are you doing out of the yard, Gerry?" Tod asked, as the dog flopped his paws all over Tod's shoulders. Of course, Gerry had been known to vault the fence, but he had not done so lately, and Tod hoped he had given up this method of departure.

"Never mind trying to soften me up," Tod scolded, but he put his arms around the dog. "I want to know why you're not in the yard where you belong."

The boys had now reached Tod, and they gathered around, and said "Hi!" But they were all busy watching Gerry, and giving him a little pat when they had a chance.

"I'll bet Ham let him out," six-year-old Barney said.

"Barney" was Bernard Uvaldi, the son of Mr. Morton's only serious rival in the men's shoe business in Baltimore. "Mr. Uvaldi is all right, but his shoes are not," was Mr. Morton's usual comment on Barney's father. Mr. Morton made the Morton Shoe in his own factory, whereas Mr. Uvaldi bought up shoes in "job lots." Sometimes they were good, but more often they were not.

"You didn't actually *see* Ham let the dog out," Charles Mattieson corrected Barney. "You just *think* he did." Charlie was Tod's best friend, and he didn't like Hamilton Calehone any better than the other boys did; but he would defend anyone or anything in the interests of fairness. At times the boys found him a nuisance, particularly when he held up a game on account of something he considered unfair.

"I betcha, I betcha it was Ham," Barney declared. "Ham's always opening the gate so that Gerry can get out. I've seen him a hunnert times." Barney looked up earnestly at Charlie through his crooked steel-rimmed spectacles.

"Aw-w, go on, a hundred times—" Charlie stopped as he saw Ham coming from the alley that ran back of Tod's house.

Although Ham was in Tod's and Charlie's class at school, he was bigger than most of his classmates. It was not because he was taller, or because he dressed and acted as much like a cowboy as he could, that Ham was disliked by the other children. It was because Ham always carried his lasso with him, and with it he was able to rope practically anything or anybody in sight. More than once he had been called before the principal for roping the younger children.

Last spring at a school picnic at Druid Hill Park, He had lassoed one of the lambs cropping grass around the Mansion House. All the boys had helped Ham disentangle the lamb for fear that their class would be blamed for it, but they were all so mad that they would have beaten Ham up if one of the teachers, ignorant of the roping, had not appeared and asked them to come and play ball.

Today Ham was dressed in his cowboy outfit, complete with hat. He was twirling his rope in a huge loop. His eyes remained intent on the rope as he

9

came down Carrollton Avenue, and as the boys approached the alley, Ham never broke the smooth rhythm of his performance.

"There's nobody in this whole city of Baltimore who can do this except me," Ham boasted. "See? Just watch me!"

"Aw—that's nothing to brag about," Barney said, lisping a little because his two front teeth were missing. "My sister does that all the time with her jump rope."

"Oh, yeah!" Ham squinted up his eyes as he thought cowboys did. "Well, she can't do this." He snaked in his lasso, looping it around his elbow, getting it ready for throwing.

Barney had seen that gesture too often not to realize that Ham was going to lasso something or somebody, and he was sure it was himself because he had dared to disagree with Ham.

Barney was taking no chances. He had so far been able to escape Ham's lasso because he could run faster than Ham could reach with his rope. So Barney raced up the alley. When he reached the safety of his own yard, he stood with the gate half open, ready to duck inside, and then gleefully stuck his tongue out at Ham.

Gerry, walking quietly beside Tod, saw the twirling rope. Immediately his muscles tensed, his nose quivered, and he stopped and leaned close to Tod. That flying rope had sometimes grazed Gerry in the past. Sensing the same threat now, Gerry suddenly

decided to leap ahead the short distance to his own gate. At that instant, the rope whipped out. It whizzed through the air, circled Gerry, and in descending caught all four of the dog's legs. Then Ham gave a quick tug, and the huge dog lost his footing. To regain his balance his claws scrabbled in the dirty, slimy gutter water, but as Ham tightened the rope, Gerry's legs were dragged from under him, and he fell over on his side with a yelp and a groan. He lay there helpless, a surprised look on his face, as if he could not understand why anyone would do such a thing to him.

"Ham!" a girl's outraged voice shrieked. "You mean old Ham-bone! How could you do that to Gerry?" It was Debbie Waid, Tod's next door neighbor, who had just come out of her gate.

"Come on!" Charlie Mattieson yelled. "We can't let Ham get away with this."

Charlie's words rallied the boys who had been standing as if frozen with shock. Some of them chased Ham and some of them ran to release Gerry, and all of them yelled at Ham as he charged up the alley with a speed he had never before achieved. The boys almost got to him, but he managed to reach his yard, dash inside, close and latch the gate, and once again escape any punishment for his cruelty.

The whole gang now became engaged in trying to loosen Gerry's bonds. They fell over one other and got into each other's way, and the dog himself hindered them by his own efforts to get up. Finally

12

Tod took the dog's big head in his arms and talked quietly to him as the boys worked.

Freed at last, Gerry stood up and gave just one indignant bark. It did not sound to Tod as if the dog were hurt, but just humiliated and insulted. His eyes had a dazed look. He held up first one front paw and then the other and he shook each one as if to see if it still worked. Then he nosed Tod's arm, and all the boys patted him.

Tod picked up the lasso that Ham had left and started to straighten it out. He wound it around his elbow as he had seen Ham do.

Gerry came and sniffed. The rope touched his nose and he smelled it with quivering nostrils. Then he growled, a real growl, and took off down the alley, racing along with the galloping stride of a pony.

"I didn't even get a chance to pat his nose," Debbie said, as she looked after him in astonishment.

Tod, too, watched until the dog turned the corner, a little puzzled at his actions.

"He never did that before, did he?" Barney asked. Barney had rejoined the group as soon as Ham was safely out of the way.

"I just wish he wasn't so independent," Tod said.

"It's all Ham's fault," Barney said.

"Do you think he'll be all right?" Debbie asked.

"Aw-w." Tod was worried himself, but he didn't want anyone to know that his dog was less than perfect. "He always comes home all right."

The boys all drifted away, even Barney. Debbie

went home and closed her gate. Tod took the lasso down to his cellar and hung it on a hook. Of course he would return it to Ham sometime, but he didn't care a bit when he did. As long as the lasso was in his cellar, Ham couldn't do any harm with it.

Tod slammed the outside cellar door as he went back into the yard. Gerry's desertion was one more thing to make him unhappy. This just wasn't his day.

He looked toward the west. Maybe there was still enough daylight for him to practice his telegraphy. Digging down into his pocket for the yellow piece of paper that had the Morse code written on it, he pulled out a piece of string, a stub of pencil, some licorice candy, some colored stones. He was sure he had it. Then out came some aggies and some almost brand-new nails he had found, and when the pocket was nearly empty, there it was—a piece of yellow paper, worn around the edges, but with the Morse alphabet still plainly visible. Holding the paper carefully, he went over to the gate latch.

Mr. Michael Treadwell had written out the alphabet for him. Mike had been manager of the Western Union Telegraph Company's branch office at Edmondson Avenue and Carey Street, and had become his friend, because Tod was always in the office begging for a job, during vacation, on weekends and even during the Christmas holidays.

After one of Mike's particularly disappointing talks with Tod, telling him why the Western Union could not take a boy so young, Tod had argued, "But

Mike, some of the Western Union messengers start at twelve years old."

"Those are all very poor boys, or else they have their family's consent," Mike answered. "Are you a *very poor* boy? Do you have your family's consent?" Because Mike smiled as he spoke, his words did not sound too severe. He looked at Tod through his big eyeglasses, rimmed in gold, and brushed back the dark lock of hair that always fell over his eye, saying, "Tell you what! I'll come and ask your father's permission for you to work on Saturdays and Sundays. How's that?"

So Mike came to call on the Mortons and met the whole family—his father and mother and his big sister, Betty Ann. Mr. Morton explained that Tod had a job waiting for him in the family shoe business. Tod was to go into the factory and the store of The Morton Shoe, and learn the business "from the ground up." In fact Tod was going to start right now, because Sales, the delivery boy, could not keep up with the deliveries, particularly on Saturdays. Telegraphy? Oh no, not for Tod. He was not to be a Western Union messenger boy, nor a telegrapher. Tod was to be a "shoe man."

When Mike saw how disappointed Tod was, he wrote out the alphabet for him. He told Tod that usually, boys got a job as a messenger, and then they had a chance to learn telegraphy. If Tod started right now to learn the Morse alphabet, he would be that much ahead.

15

So it was that on this Saturday afternoon, Tod went out to practice on the gate latch, which he had found pretty good for beating out the dots and dashes. He started with "73" because that meant "compliments" or "best regards" and it sounded nice and friendly, if anyone should be listening.

He clattered away, thinking only of dots and dashes, and all the unpleasant things of the day faded away.

He was going to be a telegraph operator. Telegraphers were given passes for ball games, free tickets for plays that came to the Academy and to Ford's Theater, and even tickets for the Circus when it came to town. Telegraphers knew everything that was going on in the world. They talked to other cities all over the country. Mike had told Tod that they could even send and receive messages between England and the United States, now that there was a transatlantic cable.

Up and down Tod snapped the gate-latch, up and down, dots and dashes, up and down. Someday he would be a telegrapher. He would talk to the whole country, to England, to the entire world. In the deepening twilight, he practiced on, dots and dashes, dots and dashes. It was almost dark when he sent out the code "30" which meant "the end."

Thoroughly satisfied that he was really remembering the Morse dots and dashes for each letter of the alphabet, Tod was feeling pretty fine, until he suddenly realized why he had been able to practice so long without interruption. It was because no Gerry had come nudging his elbow, "purring," and running the length of the yard and back, doing anything and everything to keep Tod from his telegraphy, obviously hating the click-click-click of the gate latch. Gerry had not returned, and it seemed strange to Tod not to have the big dog at his side.

2

The next morning, Tod opened his eyes and came awake with a sense of something missing. Gerry! He had not come pad-padding up the steps to wake Tod with a joyous flick of his tongue on Tod's cheek.

Gerry had not come home at all last night. He had not come for his dinner, or during the entire evening. Nor had Tod been able to find him anywhere in the neighborhood.

Tod's one hope was that he had gone down to the store, for he had done this once before when his feelings were hurt. In that case he would have come home with Mr. Morton, who always kept the store open late on Saturday nights. No Gerry at Tod's bedside in the morning meant that the dog had not come home with his father.

Tod had been tempted several times last night to telephone the store, to ask if Gerry was there. The Mortons did not have one of the "new-fangled contraptions," but there was one in another store three doors away, although Tod's father always objected strongly to the idea of being called to his neighbor's telephone.

The Mortons had no telephone at their home either, but Tod and all the Mortons were always welcome to use the Waids' telephone next door. Since Debbie's father was a doctor, they felt obliged to have a telephone, even though the reception was so poor that no one, not even the doctor, could be certain he would understand what was being said.

That was enough reason to keep Tod from the hated telephone that was trying to outdo the telegraph: never yet had he been able to understand one word that came over the instrument.

Now he washed and dressed quickly, listening all the time for a sound that could mean that Gerry had come home, but remembering to put on his Sunday clothes. Suddenly the thought came to him that Cora might have gone to early Mass and forgotten to let Gerry out of the cellar. Yet he knew that Cora never neglected Gerry.

Cora Jackson had come to live with the Morton family after the death of her husband. Other people who did not have any money were just "poor"; but because Cora came from a good family she was in "straitened circumstances." She did all the work in the big three-story house, with some help from Mrs. Morton and Betty Ann.

Tod raced downstairs and into the kitchen.

"Cora, did you let Gerry out of the cellar this morning?" he asked.

"Oh, Tod, I opened the cellar door just as I always do," Cora said, "but Gerry wasn't there. I went to the back door and called and called. Then I went to the front door and called him. He's gone! Disappeared! Vanished!" She looked at Tod sad-eyed. She loved Gerry dearly, and saved all the scraps from the table for him. She even forgave him when he walked on her just-washed floor, his big floppy paws making mud marks with each step he took.

"I was sure he would come home to sleep," Tod said. "He always does. I wonder why he didn't," Tod said in a puzzled voice.

"Who was the last one up last night? Your sister, of course, with that Mike Treadwell. She should have seen that he was in or else called some of us," Cora declared.

She went over to the big kitchen range, picked up the lid-lifter, took off the round iron stove cover and looked in at the coals. Seeing that the fire needed fuel, she banged the cover to one side, took up the coal scuttle and poured on some of the pea coal. The fire crackled and spit as she replaced the cover.

"Guess I should have come downstairs myself to make sure he was in," she said angrily, but she looked at Tod as if she were about to cry. "Oh, Tod. Poor Gerry! He's stayed out all night before but only in summer, not in freezing cold weather like this." She flopped the lid on the pot of oatmeal. "Go on in to breakfast," she said.

Tod went into the dining room to join his mother and father and Betty Ann. Cora brought in the hot oatmeal and the rich cream, the ham and the fried potatoes.

Tod said "good morning" while he wondered if his father was going to scold him about what he had said yesterday—that he "hated shoes" and did not want to deliver them.

He should have known his father better, for although Mr. Morton might be momentarily angry with him or with Betty Ann, it was soon over and he seldom referred to it again.

"Gerry always comes home, Tod." His father reached over and put his hand on Tod's arm. "So don't worry so much."

And Tod knew he had the best father in the whole world.

"I thought maybe he had gone to the store, Dad."

"No he wasn't there. I didn't see him at all."

Tod turned to his sister. "Betty Ann, didn't you see him last night? Did you call him before you went to bed?"

"Yes, I called him, Tod," Betty Ann said, but he thought she answered very slowly. "I called him. Mike went home just after Dad came in, and I went to both the front door and the back door and called him."

"Did Mike know he was gone? Why didn't you wake me? I would have gone out and looked for him," Tod said crossly.

As a sister, Betty Ann was not too bad. She was even pretty. She had brown eyes like their mother's, but this morning her eyes were red and she looked as though she had not slept too well. Her pompadour, however, was combed high on her head, as she had worn it ever since she had turned eighteen and started attending the Teacher's Training School, just up the street from them. About that time she had begun wafting her hands around as if they didn't belong to her, but Tod didn't mind because they smelled of Cashmere Bouquet soap. She and Tod usually got along fine, except at times like this morning, when it seemed to Tod that she could be awfully dumb.

"Why didn't you wake me?" Tod insisted.

"He'll come home when he wants to, son," his mother said, trying to comfort him. "You know how Gerry is. Now eat your breakfast and stop worrying."

Everyone was trying hard to be cheerful, but Tod was thinking of all the terrible things that could happen to a dog on his own in the city. They all missed the dog's funny little sighs and groans as he lay under the table, reminding them that he had not yet had *his* breakfast. No plushy dog, more like a huge rug, entangled himself in their feet so that they were afraid to move for fear of disturbing him. No cold, wet nose secretly pushed at a hand under the table, silently begging for a little something, such as a piece of ham or potato—anything, in fact, that was edible.

Tod excused himself to go out looking for Gerry as soon as he thought his father would permit it. He hurried to the front door and, remembering that it was Sunday, put on his best overcoat and his new cap that looked very grown up. He ran outside and began calling Gerry. He went down to the curbstone, and walked a little way on each side of his house. He dared not go too far from home, because his father would never agree that a lost dog was an excuse for being late for church.

It was only a few moments before his father, buttoning his heavy coat, came to the top of the steps and called to Tod. Then his mother came out smoothing her kid gloves.

"Come along, Tod," his mother said. "We'll all help you hunt for Gerry after church."

"Oh, Tod," Betty Ann was annoyed. "Come on. We'll have to rush now to get there on time." She stood in the doorway, wearing her beaver muff and fur. Her hat was of yellow and orange feathers and her brown satin dress peeped out from under her long coat and swished around her high-heeled button shoes.

Tod watched as she started down the steps, holding on to the railing of the wooden covers that were put over the marble steps every winter.

"Good thing those wooden covers are on the steps or you sure would fall and break your neck," Tod said.

"Now, Tod, you just stop teasing your sister." Cora stood at the door, with her hands folded under her apron to protect them from the cold. "There's other folks around here who are glad for these covers. I couldn't wash marble steps in this weather. The water would freeze."

As the Mortons started up the street, his mother put her arm around Tod. "Now don't worry so much, Tod. Gerry will come home all right."

"He sure will, if he isn't dead," Cora said mournfully from the top of the steps.

The family hurried along. Even with Tod lagging behind in the hope of seeing Gerry, they reached their pew a few minutes before the service started.

Tod went through the motions of kneeling, sitting down and standing up, but he had never felt less like worshiping. He looked up at the stained-glass windows that he usually enjoyed, but today there was no sun and the windows were as dark and as gloomy as his thoughts.

The choir started to sing, the congregation stood up, and Tod opened his hymn book. But he couldn't sing. It was then that he noticed an usher whisper to a man in a pew across from the Mortons, and both men hurried toward the door. In a few minutes he saw others leave their pews.

Something must have happened. His heart gave a glad leap. It must be Gerry! From the depths of his soul he prayed, "Oh, dear God, let it be Gerry!"

It would not be the first time that Gerry had

followed them to church and caused a disturbance. Gerry would not stay outside in the cold, not Gerry! He'd scratch and make a big fuss until someone let him in.

Tod craned his neck to look back at the door, but when he got a clear view, he saw that there was no dog there. Sadly, he went back to his hymn book, and tried hard to sing.

He felt that something was wrong, as more and more people left their pews.

A moment later an usher came quietly to their pew and whispered to his father. Mr. Morton picked up his black derby and followed the man to the back of the church. Tod glanced at his mother, but she was fumbling with her hymn book, trying to get it back in the rack. Betty Ann looked frightened, and her head was turned to one side as if she were trying to catch some sound.

Just then Tod heard the clanging of fire-bells. They were coming closer. He heard one engine pass, then another. He counted four engines going so fast that the pounding of the horses' hooves was like thunder on the cobblestone street.

Fire! He found he was holding his breath.

After the engines passed, there were rustlings and murmurings as people turned to each other and whispered their fears. The unrest increased, as wave after wave of anxious but hushed conversation swept through the church.

Two of the ushers hurried to the altar rail and talked to the minister in low tones. He nodded and the ushers left.

Then the minister held up his hand for silence, and all sound ceased.

"There will be no sermon this morning," he announced. "As some of you already know, there is a big fire downtown. Many of you will want to get to your places of business. God bless you all and keep you safe."

Some of the congregation were out of their pews almost before the minister had stopped speaking. Tod heard the shocked voices of the people as they hastened toward the door.

Tod and his mother and Betty Ann filed out with the others and joined Mr. Morton at the door.

"It must be an awful bad fire, Dad," Tod said.

"Well, it may not be so bad. But we all talked it over and decided it might be, so we advised the minister to cut short the services." Mr. Morton shepherded the family outside the door. Then he cleared his throat and said, "Of course, Baltimore has an excellent fire department. They can handle it."

The minister had come outside and stood on the top step with his overcoat thrown around his shoulders.

"I hope we did the right thing," the minister said. "It seemed wise to dismiss the congregation, because many of you businessmen would want to get downtown to reassure yourselves that everything is all right, if nothing else."

"Yes, yes indeed," Mr. Morton said, although he did not seem too concerned.

Tod hoped his father would go to the fire so that he could go with him. He loved to watch the firemen and the big engines and the horses.

Then he thought of Gerry. Suppose Gerry were loose somewhere in the fire? Gerry was scared to death of fire. Maybe it was his job to find Gerry and so be sure that the big dog did not wander anywhere near the fire, particularly if it was a big one.

He stood undecided with his family and noticed that no one lingered outside the church today. A few carriages were lined up against the curb, but most of the congregation had come on foot. As he turned up his overcoat collar against the cold, he saw that most of the men were doing the same thing, and that the women were pushing their hands into their muffs, just as Betty Ann was doing.

He saw a man hurrying down Carrollton Avenue, a man who looked over his shoulder every few minutes, to see if a streetcar was coming. Tod recognized Mr. Uvaldi.

"Good morning, Mr. Uvaldi." Mr. Morton said.

"Good morning, Mr. Morton." Mr. Uvaldi was a slight man and not very impressive looking, but this morning he acted very important "Did you hear? The Hurst Building blew up. Yes, sir, *blew up!*"

"The Hurst Building!" cried Mr. Morton. "How

could the Hurst Building *blow up*? You must have gotten that report over that telephone contraption, Mr. Uvaldi."

"Directly from the firemen," Mr. Uvaldi said emphatically, a little hurt that his word was being doubted. "The report came by Western Union."

"It must be true, Dad, if it came over the telegraph," Tod said.

"But the Hurst Building—that's only a few blocks from my store," Mr. Morton said.

"Not far from mine either," Mr. Uvaldi said. "I'm going down to see if everything is all right. Here comes a streetcar. Why don't you come along?"

"No," his father said, with an air of great calmness, "I'll wait and see what the later news is. It can't be as bad as you think."

As Mr. Uvaldi swung onto the street car, Tod's father said to his wife, "That Uvaldi! He always takes the worst view of everything."

"But Todhunter," Mrs. Morton said in her soft voice, "even the minister thought it might be a bad fire." She looked unruffled, except that two little worry lines had appeared between her brows, and her brown eyes had lost some of their usual serenity. Yet her hat sat at exactly the right angle, and her plum-colored suit, trimmed in mink, swung at the most fashionable fullness.

Mr. Morton stood silent for several minutes, undecided about what to do. Finally he said, "Maybe I'd better get down there. The fire seems to be pretty near the store. Of course, there's no need to worry about the factory. It's too far away."

"I think you're right, Todhunter," his mother said. "We'll hold dinner for you."

"No, don't bother, Lizzie. I'll get something to eat at the Madison House or at the Oyster House. They're both open on Sunday."

Tod knew his father was disturbed when he called his mother Lizzie instead of Elizabeth and he knew his mother must be very upset when she made no objection.

"I think, Tod, that you'd better come with me," his father said, turning to his son.

"Oh, yes, Dad, of course," Tod answered. He dismissed a fleeting thought of Gerry, for if his father needed him, then he would go with him.

"And me—me too, Dad," Betty Ann said. She loved to go to fires, where she would stand admiring the glittering fire engines and patting the big horses until the fire was over.

"You?" Mr. Morton said doubtfully. "No, I think you ought to go home with your mother."

"Oh, fudge!" Betty Ann exclaimed. "Just because I'm a girl." She kissed her mother. "You don't need me, do you, Mother?"

Mrs. Morton smiled good-naturedly, and Betty Ann grabbed her father's arm and pulled him toward the streetcar stop. Tod hesitated and then was about to follow them, when he felt his mother's arm around his shoulders.

"You're worried about Gerry, aren't you?" she said.

His mother always seemed to know when something was bothering him. She understood that he wanted to go with his father to help him if necessary, but that by so doing he was deserting his dog.

"When I heard all the commotion in church, I thought it was Gerry, and that he had followed us," Tod told her.

"Tod, dear, suppose you go along with your father and I will go out and try to find Gerry?" his mother suggested.

He couldn't help smiling. His mother running around alleys looking for Gerry suddenly seemed very funny to him and he laughed.

"Dressed up like that?" he asked.

"Cora will help me hunt and maybe some of the children. I'll talk to Debbie as soon as I get home," his mother said. "How about Ham?" She paused. Tod had told her about Ham throwing Gerry into the gutter.

"Ham?" Tod exploded. "That Ole Hambone? After the way he treated Gerry? I think that's why Gerry didn't come home."

"Maybe that's all the more reason that we should let Ham know what happened."

"Mother," Tod said earnestly, "do you think that Ham could have taken Gerry and locked him up overnight just to scare me?"

"Now, Tod, don't imagine things," his mother

said. "Of course, Ham should never have roped and thrown poor Gerry that way. But I doubt if Ham or anyone else could push or pull that dog and make him go anywhere he didn't want to go. No, Tod, we'll just have to think of where the dog would go of his own accord."

"Well, the store is the only place I can think of," Tod said.

"Yes, the store, that's right," his mother said, after thinking for a moment. "He likes that old rug in the back room, doesn't he? And sometimes that door gets closed on him—"

The streetcar was nearing the stop. His mother gave him a little push. "Go on," she said.

Tod pecked a kiss in the general direction of his mother's cheek.

" 'Bye," he called.

"Tod!" cried his mother and grabbed his arm to stop him. Her face was very white. "Stop your father! Stop him!" Then, not waiting for Tod to act, she picked up her voluminous skirts and ran to where Mr. Morton and Betty Ann waited for the car. "Todhunter! Todhunter!" she shouted, disregarding all the rules about ladies behaving quietly on the streets.

"Todhunter," she said, when she reached the corner, "could you have closed Gerry in that back room in the store last night? The little room with that rug he likes? Oh, Todhunter, did you see him at all last evening? If he was in that back room—oh,

Todhunter, could he get out if the fire came close? Oh, Todhunter, did you see him *at all* yesterday?"

"No, no, Lizzie, I didn't see him but you know how independent he is. He comes and goes as he pleases."

The streetcar came rumbling up to the corner. Mr. Morton motioned for Betty Ann and Tod to get on. "We'll get down there as fast as possible. Now don't worry, Lizzie. He'll be all right. If he's in the store, he may be a little frightened, but the store won't burn down—at least—well, we'll get down there right away. Now don't worry!"

He climbed aboard the car and waved back at Mrs. Morton.

3

As the Mortons took seats in the streetcar, Tod thought his father looked very worried. It was as if the possibility that he had locked Gerry in the store had been the thing that made him suddenly conscious of all the terrible things that could happen in a fire. When the conductor came and collected three nickles for their fares, Mr. Morton did not make his usual jokes about Tod's no longer being a "child" who could ride for three cents. He sat grim and silent.

There were not many people aboard when the Mortons got on, but more passengers came into the car at each corner. Most of them had something to say about the fire, but nobody seemed to know anything definite about it.

"Don't worry, Tod," his father finally said. "I doubt if Gerry is in the store. It's possible he could have sneaked into the back room without my seeing him, but I don't think so."

"I sure hope he didn't," Tod said. "Even if he is so big, he's awfully afraid of fire."

"He may smell smoke, and he may be frightened," Mr. Morton said, "but probably nothing will happen to him. The fire, even if it's bad, can hardly reach the store before we get there."

Still more people boarded the car, and each person seemed to have some alarming tale to tell about the fire. These stories frightened the passengers and made them more and more fidgety. Tod could see how nervous everyone was and how anxious to get downtown quickly.

Betty Ann had looked sad and sort of unhappy all morning even before they had heard of the fire.

"Betty Ann, maybe we could stop at the Equitable Building and see Mike," Tod said, trying to cheer her up. Mike had been promoted from the Edmondson Avenue branch office to the main office of the Western Union. Mike would know how bad the fire was because information always came pouring into the Western Union.

To Tod's surprise, Betty Ann looked more unhappy than ever at the mention of Mike's name.

"Well"—she seemed reluctant to talk—"well," she said slowly, and then burst out, "we had a fight last night before Dad came home." She sounded close to tears.

"A *fight?*" Tod said. How could she possibly fight with Mike? "What did you fight about?"

"Oh, everything," she said vaguely. She stuck her nose in the air and Tod knew he would get no more out of her.

Mike was Tod's very best friend—the one he looked up to and admired. After meeting Betty Ann, however, Mike had started talking so much to her that Tod was often left out of the conversation entirely. Lately Mike had been taking Betty Ann to dinner and to the theater, without even asking Tod to go along. Mike's invitations were always last-minute arrangements, because telegraphers never knew in advance when they could have time off, and they always worked on Saturdays and Sundays.

Tod knew that Mike would be working today, and probably harder than ever because of the fire. If he and Betty Ann could get to the Western Union office, Mike would have all the news on the fire. Tod could imagine the main office humming with the story, BIG FIRE IN BALTIMORE, or something equally startling.

They would need extra messengers! The thought suddenly struck Tod. "Betty Ann!" he caught his sister's arm. "The Western Union will need messengers, lots of them to carry messages. I'm going to see Mike. If I could make good during this fire, I'd be able to have a job next summer."

"What is this nonsense?" Mr. Morton asked. Tod had thought his father was not paying any attention to what he said. "Your job is waiting for you at The Morton Shoe. Sales really needs help on Saturdays."

"Sales!" Betty Ann broke in with her very special tone of distaste. "I wonder why you still keep Sales, after all we've heard about his trying to get jobs with other shoe stores. You just can't trust that Vincent deSales Donnella." She dragged out his full name, even though no one ever called him anything but Sales.

"You just don't like him." Tod felt his anger rising. He was very fond of Sales. He liked his good humor, and admired his hard work, and his care for his widowed mother, with whom he lived. She was housekeeper for Mrs. Sattfield, a friend of the Mortons. Tod had quarrelled with Betty Ann many times about Sales. "You're against him because he's a foreigner," Tod said, and he knew he was talking too loudly. "Only he isn't. He was born here."

The streetcar jerked to an abrupt stop to allow a fire engine to pass in front of it. Everyone in the car was jolted, and those who were standing in the aisle were piled up toward the front.

A man jumped on the moving car just as it got under way again. His eyes were red and his clothes gave off a smoky smell. His voice was frightened. "Engines coming from Relay—even from Washington," he said.

The conductor pushed through the car. "Can't say how far we'll go," he announced, in an excited voice. "Baltimore Street has hose all over it. Fayette Street may be closed next."

Passengers seemed stunned for a moment. The man across from the Mortons was holding the Sunday *Sun*, as if he were reading it, but he never moved the paper, or turned a page. Tod saw the date— February 7, 1904.

Several people got on the car. "The whole city could go," one of them said.

"Baltimore has an excellent fire department," Mr. Morton said to no one in particular. He had said this more than once and Tod hoped it was true.

Tod wanted to ask his father if he had bought Gerry's new license, because the old one was out of date. His father had been promising to get it, and then forgetting it, ever since the first of the year. Now, with a fire raging, Gerry's license was particularly important because the dog might be hurt, or picked up by the Society for the Prevention of Cruelty to Animals, or even by the police. Tod wanted to ask his father about it. It had been in his mind ever since they had left the church, but his father had seemed so preoccupied and looked so depressed that Tod hated to add to his burdens. He heaved a sigh and said nothing.

Outside the windows of the car, Tod had been noticing little puffs of smoke for some time, and now light gossamer clouds began to invade the interior. At first the small amount of smoke that seeped in was hardly noticeable, but then it thickened and became a blue-white haze. Tod coughed and Betty Ann buried her face in her muff. Other passengers began to choke and cough.

Tod saw through the windows that groups of sightseers, sometimes whole families, were held back by the police at the street corners. Fire engines were lined up against the curb, and more of them were dashing up—to come to a standstill when faced with a street clogged with hose that snaked all over the cobblestones.

He could see the motorman through the front door, as he peered through the smoke that was turning darker each minute, and closing down over the car like a smothering curtain that gradually hid the car tracks, the street and everything else in front of the vehicle. The motorman brought the car to a stop, swung the handle around, and cut off the power. Then he took out his hankerchief and mopped his eyes. Forlornly he turned and opened the door.

"Far as we go, folks," he said to the passengers.

The people rose silently. Too shocked to utter a word of protest at the abrupt ending of their ride, they filed into the smoke-filled street.

Tod thought he knew every corner and every landmark on the Carey Street car line. But when the three Mortons stepped from the car, they were in a world where smoke blotted out stores, houses and signs. Tod knew they were on Fayette Street but that was all he was sure of.

The fire, the smoke and the crowds were bad enough, but what bothered Tod most was the holiday air of some of the sightseers. Dressed in their best clothes, families seemed to have brought all their children, even the very small ones. Fathers often acted as guides. "Now you look down that street there, and you can see the flames," one father directed.

The car had left them far from the store. Mr. Morton talked of various routes to get there and finally decided they must veer to the north and go around the fire. He was calm, but Tod read in his father's face an awareness of the danger that had not been there before.

"We must hurry," he said.

The Mortons passed Lexington Market. After several blocks they turned east. Tod noticed that as they came closer to the fire, people had lost their holiday air and bystanders had begun to help the property owners to save their possessions. Women and children were being led away from the fire, and policemen were warning people to leave the area unless they had business there. Everywhere there seemed to be a certainty that the fire would come and they must save what they could.

Tod saw that many of the hoses were in shreds and had been abandoned in the streets. As the Mortons hesitated at a corner, a hose just beyond them burst under too much pressure, exploding a geyser of water and drenching everyone the length of a half block. Live embers blew crazily in the wind. A newspaper caught fire and was blown down the center of the street. Black ashes made clouds of smoking soot that settled and covered everything like a suffocating blanket.

"Wet your handkerchiefs," said Mr. Morton, and Tod took BettyAnn's with his and spread them above a leaky hose. "You may need them to breathe through. Keep them ready," his father warned, as he led the way. "Stay close behind me."

At the next corner, they saw a fireman, holding a pair of fire horses. Both animals had been singed, and one had a badly burned leg. Their eyes looked scared, but they stood quietly.

"We'd just brought up the fire engine," the fireman told the crowd that had gathered around them, "didn't even have the horses unhitched, when the Hurst Building went up like a volcano—bricks, mortar, broken glass all came down on top of us. Goliath* here had his leg burned, but he stood there. The horses never moved," he declared proudly.

Firemen were always brave, Tod knew, but this one looked ready to cry as he wrapped his handkerchief around Goliath's burned leg and led him off. Tod's throat choked up. What was happening was bad enough for people—but for animals it must hold a greater terror. Tod thought of Gerry, who might be locked in the store, not understanding why he had been deserted. Or perhaps Gerry was wandering the smoky streets, bewildered and lost.

"You shouldn't bring those young people in here," a policeman said to his father. Like all the policemen in Baltimore, he was very big and full of

* Goliath lived for many years afterward.

42

authority in the frock coat of his blue uniform and the large helmet with gold insignia.

"I need my son and daughter to help me save things from my store. We think maybe our dog is locked in the store, too."

"You're Mr. Morton, aren't you?" the policeman peered at him and then smiled broadly. "Sure and it's Gerry you're talking about? Nothing to worry about. Gerry is so big that if he gets bored with being locked in, he'll just tear the door down." The man laughed at his own joke, then became confidential, and gave them all the information that he thought would be helpful.

"Now the streets down that way are lined with fire engines, packed solid at some spots. You'll have to go around, maybe Charles Street will be open."

"How did it happen so fast?" Mr. Morton asked. "Hurst had automatic fire alarms in his building. Didn't they work?"

"They worked when the fire got to them," the policeman said. "It looks like the fire smoldered all night in some blankets in the basement. The fire alarm went off only a few minutes before the building blew up!"

"*Why* did it blow up?"

"Smoke explosion. And then the fire fanned out. It's between here and your store now, Mr. Morton."

"Then how do I get my things out?"

A fireman, uncoiling hose next to the policeman, laughed somberly.

"A thousand people would like to know the answer to that one right now," the fireman said. "Maybe you *don't* want to take things from your store. Some are saying that if part of the stock is removed, none of the insurance on the stock can be collected."*

"Unless you can move all of your stock of shoes, maybe you'd better let it all stay," the policeman said, trying to be helpful.

"Some things I *must* get," Mr. Morton said. "Saturday's cash, my files and my records. The insurance policies are in my safe deposit box at the Savings Bank of Baltimore."

"Banks all have time locks!" the policeman said. "None of the vaults will open until Monday morning, that is if they don't burn up."

"Pretty bad, isn't it?" Mr. Morton said. "Do you think our fire department can handle it?"

"We're getting volunteers to carry coal for the engines and to move extra hose. We've sent to Washington and to New York for help. Washington firemen can get here quickly on the B.&.O. Western Union says they're loading hose in New York for us, in the aisles of the passenger trains."

Western Union! Tod thought of Mike in the Main Office!

Resolutely the Mortons turned toward Charles

---

* Confusion over the exact meaning of the insurance policies continued all through the fire.

Street. Betty Ann put her handkerchief over her mouth and took hold of Tod's arm as they struggled along after their father.

"I shouldn't have brought you two into this," Mr. Morton shouted over his shoulder. "Maybe you'd better go back, both of you—"

They motioned that they were going with him as they pushed past people pulling loaded carts and children's wagons. They gasped as the wind lifted a paper from a wheelbarrow being trundled along the gutter. The wheelbarrow was loaded with stacks of money, mostly ten- and twenty-dollar bills. A gust of wind caught up the contents of the wheelbarrow and suddenly money was floating all around in the air. Some of it was grabbed and returned to the owner. Many people were too frantic even to bother reaching out to grasp the money. Tod could hear shouting and cursing, and praying and crying.

Suddenly Betty Ann giggled. Her father looked at her sternly and Tod wondered if she were getting hysterical. She pointed to a man walking solemnly down the center of the street.

The man was dressed as if he had just come from church, even to his high silk hat. He walked steadily and unhurriedly with his raised umbrella held over his head to fend off the flaming embers from the sky. The awful thing was that the cloth of the umbrella had been burned away completely, leaving only the steel ribs that were no protection at all.

Their attention was caught by a fireman who

45

had evidently been off duty when the fire started, and who was handling hose in his "Sunday best." When his partner saw a piece of burning paper settle on his shoulder, he turned the fire hose on him. The man, drenched, his teeth chattering, wiped water from his face and sputtered furiously.

"You idiot! You didn't have to drown me just to put out a spark!"

"Didn't I?" The man holding the nozzle guffawed. "One second more and you'd have been wearing a bonfire around your neck. The spark was right next to that new celluloid collar of yours! That stuff is as explosive as gunpowder!"

"Glory!" The man put his hand to his throat. "Celluloid! I forgot I still had that on." He yanked the collar from his neck and threw it on the ground and stamped on it. "My wife warned me that it could blow up!"

"Risking your life to cut down a laundry bill!"

Pushing and shoving as best they could, the Mortons went on their way. They were well to the north of the fire, and turned south to come down Charles Street. Then they heard a word, a word that shocked them so much that they stood motionless and silent, touched by a fear they had never before known.

"Dynamite!" a voice in the crowd shouted. "They're going to use dynamite."

4

The harsh word "dynamite" roared through the crowd. Women screamed it, men cursed it. An old fellow running down the middle of Charles Street seemed crazed with fear as he shrilled, "Run! Run! Run for your lives! They're going to dynamite all the buildings!"

"Why should they do that?" Betty Ann had to shriek to be heard. "Why should they use dynamite?"

"To destroy everything in the path of the fire, so it has nothing to feed on," Mr. Morton explained. "It is always a last resort. They must be convinced there's no other way to stop it. But there's no reason to panic! They would never use it without warning."

Wouldn't they? Tod thought. The way everyone had suddenly gone crazy, who could tell what would happen?

Dynamite! The store might by dynamited, even if it did not burn down. And no one would look, would they, for a sad-eyed dog locked in the building? Of course not. Gerry's only hope was for them to get to the store as fast as possible.

People were spilling out of Clay Street, yelling

as they ran, "Dynamite! Dynamite!" Tod saw that this little alley off Charles Street was backed with wagons and drays. Evidently the drivers had thought it a safe place, where they could wait for a load to carry away from the fire. Tod saw that the drivers were having a harder and harder time controlling their horses in the jammed alleyway, and horses and drivers became more nervous as the excitement increased. When the dread word "dynamite" came, every driver—his wagon packed wheel against wheel —grabbed his whip and urged his horse forward into a space that did not exist.

Screaming, rearing horses pulled up high, pounded the air with their hooves, as crashing wagon wheels smacked against each other. Shouts and curses and groans came from the drivers, and over and above all the noise came the panic-stricken voices yelling "Dynamite! Dynamite!"

The Mortons clung to each other. Tod was afraid they would never get past the alley. Yet they had to continue down Charles Street if they were ever to reach the store. To go any round-about way now would take too much time.

Then Mr. Morton strode toward the alley, and Tod knew he was going to pass in front of those frantic horses. He and Betty Ann held tight to each other as they tried to follow their father.

Mr. Morton made a wedge of his shoulders to force a path through the crowd for himself and his children. His coat was sprinkled with dust and ashes and his face smeared with soot, but he went marching along. It came to Tod that his father was a courageous man and he expected his children to be brave, too.

"Here we go! Here we go!" their father kept saying. Yet there was never any opening ahead, only a swirling mass of men and horses and wagons. "Here we go!" he said again, and they were off the curb and pushing, scrambling, fighting their way across Clay Street.

They had almost reached the other side, when Tod heard over and above the sound of horses' hooves and wagon wheels, shouts of alarm, high and hysterical, and a pair of enormous grays, hitched to a dray, broke free and dashed wildly toward the street.

Mr. Morton grabbed Tod and Betty Ann, one in each hand, and gave a tremendous heave, and hauled them like two sacks of potatoes, stumbling and sprawling, onto the safety of the sidewalk.

"Are you all right? Sorry I had to be so rough," he shouted as he helped them to their feet.

Tod was so shaken he could hardly speak. Betty Ann tried to smile but Tod saw that she was ready to cry.

They stood looking at each other and trying to get their breath, and then started to walk south again. After they had passed Clay Street, they found less people—only a few men intent on their own business. Betty Ann seemed to be the only woman.

"Dad! Dad!" Betty Ann suddenly struck her father on the head with her muff, knocking off the black derby. Tod thought she had gone crazy.

As the hat fell to the ground, an ember perched on the top of it burst into flamcs, and then rolled off onto the redbrick pavement. The hat had a round hole burned in it as big as a silver dollar. They stared at it in disbelief, as Betty Ann smoothed her beaver muff.

"Oh," said their father. "Good thing you knocked it off, Betty Ann. I didn't know what had happened for a moment." He picked up his hat and put it back on his head. "Guess I'd better wear it so I won't take cold," he said in a voice that he tried to make matter-of-fact.

Soot sifted down on his face, flushed to a bright red from his exertions. Dust lay in patches on his coat, and it looked as if some small holes had been burned in it.

"Come on!" Mr. Morton urged, as he began to walk faster. He was thoroughly alarmed now. "The records! We must save those, even if other things are lost."

They began to run, but were soon slowed down as they climbed over fallen signs and cornices, and picked their way around piles of smoking rubble. Then, only a block away, they saw the store standing bravely in the midst of all the chaos, with the sign above the door: The Morton Shoe.

They had made it!

Mr. Morton rushed forward, with Tod and Betty Ann following. The policeman on duty did not recognize them.

"I'm Morton," their father said.

"I wouldn't have known you." The policeman shook his head. "Better get out of here quickly, Mr. Morton."

"I must get my things from the safe—cash—my records—files—" He headed for the door.

"And Gerry! Gerry, too!" Nobody paid any attention to Tod's shouts.

"You can't go in there," the policeman said as he took Mr. Morton's arm. A fireman grasped his other arm and together they held him.

"Don't try to stop me," their father said. "I've come all this way through the fire. Nobody can keep me out of my own store."

There was a rumble like the sound of a million hoofbeats. Policemen came running with a rope and pushed everyone back behind it. The crowd gave way slowly, fascinated by the flames that licked and leaped behind "The Morton Shoe" sign. A frightful pounding filled the air.

"There she goes!" a fireman yelled.

Every door and window filled suddenly with shooting flames, and the building seemed to explode. For a moment the russet shoes, sitting proudly beside the patent leather and vici kids, showed smartly in the brilliant light. Then the roof and walls and floors fell in an avalanche of planks and bricks and mortar, and buried sign and all—everything that had been The Morton Shoe.

The policeman and fireman still held their father, but they were no longer restraining him, they were holding him up.

"Sorry, Mr. Morton. Sorry." It was all they seemed able to say. They led him around the corner where he could sit on the curbstone but could no longer see the destruction.

Tod and Betty Ann followed. Betty Ann, mopping tears as she went, sat down beside her father. Tod moved to sit on the other side, but a man slid into the place. It was Mr. Uvaldi, and he was as red-eyed and smudged as they were.

Mr. Uvaldi sat down and laid his hand on Mr. Morton's knee. The rivals looked at each other. Mr. Uvaldi spoke first.

"My store burned up too," he said.

Mr. Morton put his hand over Mr. Uvaldi's. Sitting on the curbstone in the ruins, the two men clasped hands, as if in this way they could share each other's grief.

Tod knelt on the sidewalk behind his father. He put his arm around his father's neck and hugged him fiercely.

It was all over. They had not saved the stock or the records or even the cash from the Saturday sales. Their dangerous trip had been in vain.

Tod put his face close to his father's and cried as he had never cried before. He was just discovering how much he cared, not just for the building where they sold shoes, but for something much more important: his contentment in the achievements of his family, his father and his grandfather, and his pride in the success of his father's hard work, of The Morton Shoe.

5

They sat close together, around the corner from where the store had been—Tod and Betty Ann, Mr. Morton and Mr. Uvaldi. The curbstone on which they sat, at a distance from the crowds, seemed an island of refuge.

Tod was not the only one who had cried. Mr. Morton and Mr. Uvaldi wiped their eyes unashamedly. Betty Ann, whose wisp of a handkerchief was of little use, had simply sobbed into her muff.

Mr. Uvaldi's store was gone. Mr. Morton's store was gone. Tod saw that his father was making a great effort to appear as usual, but his hands shook, and his face was twitching. Tod had never realized until now how much he loved his father. Mr. Morton was a man sure of himself, confident and successful. Tod muffled a sob as he remembered that he had failed his father in the only big thing his father had ever demanded of him—to deliver shoes.

Tod vowed to himself that he would never again fail his father, that he would never forget how much he loved him. He could even love The Morton Shoe. Deep down in his heart, Tod knew he had always felt this way, but he hoped that this did not mean that he must always deliver shoes instead of messages.

"Guess that's all the time out for crying that we can take." Mr. Morton tried to speak in his everyday brisk way. "We'll get over this." His eyes looked blank, though, as he mopped his face with his soot-stained handkerchief. He kept saying, "We'll get over this," in a hoarse voice.

Tod and Betty Ann exchanged frightened glances. Could their father build another store? Their father and their father's father had worked all their lives establishing The Morton Shoe. No wonder he was shattered by his loss. Other stores and businesses had gone up in flames, but the fire was still raging out of control, and who knew what would be left of the city of Baltimore when the fire was finally extinguished?

Right now the question was what they did next. The factory? It was a large and well equipped building. Maybe Dad could set up some sort of temporary headquarters in it, until he could find a new store. They would all help.

"The fire is worse," a policeman spoke to them, his voice full of sympathy. "We are clearing the whole district. Sorry, but you'll have to move, Mr. Morton—you and Mr. Uvaldi."

"Yes, we'll have to move." Mr. Morton made an effort to rise but the policeman had to help him to his feet. He took off his soot-covered hat, that had a hole in the top, and started to wipe the sweatband with his handkerchief. When he saw how black and filthy they both were, he shook his head despairingly, and put the hat back on his head.

"We're here," he said, "we're alive. That's the important thing. I came down here to save my business and I'm lucky to come out with my children, safe and sound. The worst loss is the records. They go back to the day the business started. If only I could have saved those."

"I lost mine, too," Mr. Uvaldi said quietly.

The policeman looked at Betty Ann. "Your father has had a big shock," he said. "Better get him away from here as fast as you can. It's getting worse every minute."

"Officer," Mr. Morton said, "did you by any chance see a big dog anywhere?" So his father had not forgotten Gerry!

"Oh," the policeman smiled, "you mean Gerry? No, I didn't, but I haven't been on duty long. I know Gerry all right, but he couldn't possibly have been in the store or he would have howled." Then the policeman looked embarrassed, as he added, "I think."

"I *think*," the policeman had said. Tod remembered the horrible crashing and crumbling of the explosion. Would anyone have heard Gerry, even if he had howled?

"Better get started and go toward the east." The policeman hurried them along. "And I wouldn't loiter."

"Shouldn't we go to the factory?" Betty Ann said. The feathers on her gay little hat were singed in places, and her muff was bedraggled, but her chin was lifted bravely.

"The factory? yes, yes. Of course, of course." Mr. Morton seemed vague and his repeating so much frightened Tod. Now, however, he turned to Betty Ann and tried to smile a little as he said, "You're sure you don't mind?"

"Oh, Dad," she said, and she grabbed his arm affectionately.

Tod put his hand through his father's other arm, and together he and Betty Ann tried to keep him from looking back where only a jagged corner of a wall remained to show where the store had been. Nothing else was to be seen except a flickering flame above a heap of mortar, bricks and rubble.

"My wife," Mr. Uvaldi said and stopped to catch his breath. He had been trailing behind, seeking a street that seemed open so he could cut to the north and get home. "My wife doesn't know the store is gone," he said sadly.

"Neither does mine," Mr. Morton said in a surprised sort of way, as if he could hardly believe it himself. He stopped walking, and said in a hesitant way, "I'd rather tell her myself. But maybe, maybe you could tell her that we are all all right, yes, all right, and that the store is gone," his words trailed off faintly, and then he said loud and clear, "and we'll be home soon, yes, soon."

Mr. Uvaldi started to say "goodbye" but Mr. Morton began to talk slowly and clearly.

"I guess I'm better off than you are, Uvaldi. I've still got my factory. When the fire is over, come to see me, and we'll work something out."

Tod felt a surge of relief. Even though his father was upset, his mind was working, and he was planning for the future.

Mr. Uvaldi looked at his father gratefully, his relief showing on his face. He seemed unable to speak as he wrung Mr. Morton's hand. With a "goodbye" and a fervent "thank you," he started to walk north.

The three Mortons went on in the direction of the factory. Soot continued to land on their foreheads and cheeks, and the flying sparks made them conscious that their clothing was probably dotted with tiny holes.

Tod peered down every street and alleyway, looking for Gerry. He knew that dogs do not linger where there is fire, and he hoped that Gerry was far from it, but he wished he knew *where*. Could Gerry possibly have been in the store when it blew up?

Plodding wearily through the smoke-darkened streets, with a hot wind fanning their necks, they were a long time reaching the manufacturing district. As they neared Gay Street, Tod saw men carrying things from their business places, although there was no fire here. When they turned the corner, The Morton Shoe factory stood solid and dependable and *safe*. Mr. Morton stopped a moment, lifted his head and stared at it.

"There is something beside the front door," Mr. Morton said.

Tod saw it and so did Betty Ann. It looked like four wheels and a handle, topped by a heap of old clothes. Then they saw a tall, thin figure braced against the door frame.

"It's Sales!" Betty Ann exclaimed in a hushed voice. "And do you see what he is holding on to? Tod's old baby carriage."

"Oh, no," her father said, with panic in his voice.

"You remember that Mother had it put in the basement hoping to find someone who needed it?" Sheer amazement silenced them all for a moment, and then Betty Ann said, "What do you suppose he has in it?"

"Nothing of any account, surely. He couldn't get to the really valuable things because they are all in the safe." Mr. Morton groaned. "If he's carted away shoes, he may have invalidated the whole insurance, because they may not pay off if any of the stock is taken off the premises." His sigh was heavy with discouragement. "And for those few pairs of shoes, I may lose thousands of dollars worth of insurance."

Tod ran ahead to the factory. When he reached Sales and grabbed his arm, he saw that the delivery boy was shaking all over. His lips and hands were blue with cold, and his eyes were feverishly bright. He was dirty and grimy with soot.

"I waited at the store," Sales said. "I thought Mr. Morton would surely come. Then when it got too dangerous, I came to the factory. I knew you'd come, Mr. Morton, as soon as you could." Sales' voice was scratchy and wheezy. "My mother tried to make me stay home because of this cold I have, but I was sure you'd need me."

Tod felt very guilty. Sales, in spite of his cold, had come down to help the Mortons, yet he had worked until around midnight, the night before, making deliveries. Tod knew that Sales' workload was heavier than ever because Tod had not been there to help him.

"The store, Tod, the beautiful store, did it go?" Sales asked.

Tod nodded.

"Oh, I am sorry," Sales said. "You couldn't save any of the shoes?"

"No," Tod said.

He saw the glisten of tears in the Italian boy's eyes, and realized how deeply he had loved the store. As Mr. Morton and Betty Ann came up to them, Tod whispered to Sales, "It has been a terrible shock to Dad."

His father greeted Sales and gave him a half-hearted smile. "Hello, Sales, so you came down."

Betty Ann greeted Sales also, and then exclaimed, "Why, you silly boy, putting your overcoat over that old baby carriage, and you've already got a cold!"

Tod had a strong urge to talk about the store. "Everything went, Sales, everything. The store—it just blew up. And Sales, the records, they're all gone—"

Sales tried to say something but was stopped by a fit of coughing; he managed only a sound like a croak, as he waved his arms around, and pointed to the baby carriage. When he spoke his voice was scarcely more than a whisper, and all the Mortons could make out was that he had brought the baby carriage and its contents from the store.

"Don't try to talk for a minute, Sales. You've got a terrible cold. I'll tell you about things. We lost the records in the fire and that was worse even than losing all the cash, several hundred dollars, Dad thinks. And Sales, Sales, *we've lost Gerry!*" And with that Tod cried openly and unashamedly.

"No. Wait." Sales made a great effort. "Wait," he commanded in a voice that sounded like the creak of a rusty hinge. "About Gerry. He's all right, at least he was when I saw him last. I told you the policeman let me use my key to go into the store. Or did I forget that? Anyhow, it was not until I got into the store that Gerry let out a roar, but he hadn't made a sound until he heard me. He was in that little back room with the nice soft rug. Someone had closed the door on him. Guess they didn't see him." Sales coughed and couldn't go on for a moment. "Well, I opened the door, and Gerry came out and said "hello" very nicely, by licking my ear and purring as loud as one of those new automobiles. Then he ran out of the store as fast as he could. I didn't see him again but I'm sure he is all right." Sales smiled, his teeth showing white against his olive skin.

So Gerry was safe. It was the first bit of good news they had heard since leaving the church. Of course, they didn't know where he was, but at least he had not been locked in the store when it caught fire.

"He'll go right home now, I'm sure," Tod said, but he wasn't sure. After Gerry's act of tearing away from the alley last night, he didn't know what Gerry might do.

"Poor Gerry," Betty Ann said, "I hope he wasn't too scared. And it was you who rescued him, Sales," she said softly. Tod was happy that she seemed to have gotten over her suspicions about the dreamy-eyed Italian, now that he had shown his loyalty to the Mortons.

His father patted Sales on the back in an absent-minded way, trying his best to be nice to him in spite of the fact that the laden baby buggy might cheat the Mortons out of a great deal of money, just for a few pairs of salvaged shoes.

"Well, Sales," his father said, "you certainly *tried*." His father glanced at the baby buggy and Tod realized that his father really did not *care* what was in it, because all the valuable things had been in the safe.

"I needed something to put these things in," Sales croaked, "and I remembered Tod's buggy for a bambino so I got it up from the cellar, but the police and the firemen kept yelling at me to get out, because they were afraid the store would blow up—"

"Let's get inside out of the cold," Mr. Morton said, taking his keys from his pocket.

Tod took hold of the handle of the baby carriage to help Sales push it into the factory.

The door on the ground floor of the factory opened directly into the stockroom, one corner of which was used as an office for the wholesale business. Along the walls ran rows of shelves on which stood the newly finished shoes waiting to be placed pair by pair in boxes marked The Morton Shoe.

As Tod shoved the baby carriage up to the desk, the factory seemed strangely silent without the clatter of the machines heard on week-days.

"Dad, please." Betty Ann looked at her father, a worried little frown on her face. "Please, Dad, sit down and rest. Let me take your overcoat." She took his overcoat as he dropped heavily into his desk chair.

"Give me your coat, too," she said to Sales. "You should never have taken it off to cover up the shoes in that old carriage. You'll catch your death of cold."

"Shoes?" said Sales blankly. "Shoes? You think that I have *shoes* in the buggy?"

"Haven't you?" said Betty Ann.

"I would have liked to take some shoes," Sales said, "but it was not possible."

"What *have* you got, then?" Mr. Morton suddenly showed interest.

Sales lifted the overcoat from the baby carriage. He ticked off the contents of the buggy on his fingers, his hoarse voice becoming a little stronger as he talked.

"I have the cashbox with all the money, including what came in on Saturday night. I have the store records, and the names and addresses of all the supply houses and of all the regular customers. I don't know what else I have. I just emptied everything into the buggy, Mr. Morton." Sales grinned happily as the Mortons stared at him, speechless.

6

"Oh, Sales!" Betty Ann gasped.

"Thank Heavens!" Mr. Morton looked like a man who had just seen a miracle.

"Sales!" Tod was so proud of his friend that he could not find words good enough to praise him. "You're—well, you're wonderful! First you save Gerry and then you save everything in the safe."

But the mystery of how Sales got into the safe was still unexplained. Mr. Morton was so busy leafing through the contents of the baby buggy that it was several minutes before he looked at Sales in happy bewilderment.

"Everything is here," Mr. Morton said. "Everything that I need to keep me in business, as long as the factory can still produce shoes." He threw his arms around Sales and hugged him, and then said, a little puzzled, "But Sales, how did you ever get the safe open? I know you had the key to the store, but the safe was a secret combination."

"Mr. Morton, I've known that combination for a long time. How could I help it? I watched you every morning, and I couldn't help but learn it." Sales stopped for a moment, racked by his cough. "Today, I waited for you to come. Then the police said it was getting more and more dangerous, and that I would have to get out. So I just went ahead and opened it— yes, without permission, and I take the blame for it. I couldn't save your store for you, but I thought if you had your records, and the cash, you could still stay in business."

"I can," said Mr. Morton, "and I will, too." His smile for Sales was rare and special, and his blue eyes had the look of summer skies after a storm. "I'll show my gratitude to you later, Sales. We'll have another store and you will be a salesman. Right now, I think you should go home, boy. Get some rest and let your mother take care of you, and don't come out again until you are over that cold."

"I'd rather stay here," Sales insisted.

"Take a few days' vacation," Mr. Morton said firmly. He was now recovered and in full command of the situation. "We'll get reorganized and I'll continue the business from here. We will use part of this storeroom for our retail shop."

Sales finally left, his cold so bad that he could not out-talk them. He was smiling happily, now that he was sure that the factory of The Morton Shoe was safe.

"Think of that boy using his overcoat to protect these papers from the fire," Mr. Morton said, still a little dazed as he watched Sales leave the factory.

"And I thought he had no loyalty," Betty Ann

said thoughtfully. "Well, all I can do is to try to be more decent than ever to him, and try to show him how grateful we all are, and how much we trust him."

"That's my girl," Mr. Morton said, and he was almost cheerful. He walked over to the window, and stood looking out with his hands clasped in back of him.

"There's Mr. Flint, from next door. He seems to be just getting down here." He watched for a few minutes and then said, "I think I'll go talk to him. Maybe he will know more about these insurance policies. Mine are locked up in the safe deposit box at the Savings Bank of Baltimore."

"Dad," Tod said, "while you are gone, suppose Betty Ann and I cover up the shoes on the shelves, if you'll tell us where there is some canvas. It's going to be mighty dirty around here for the next few days."

His father looked his surprise at Tod's interest in the shoes. Had it taken this catastrophe to make Tod appreciate the family business? He said nothing, as he motioned Tod to the next room where the canvas was.

"Dad," Tod said, as his father left, "you'll be back soon, won't you? Because I want to go and see Mike and get him to send a messenger boy to ask Mother if Gerry got home all right."

"Why not try the telephone, Tod?" Betty Ann said with an impish grin.

"The *telephone!*" Tod reacted as she had expected. "*Telephones* won't be working." Then he added grandly, "Only the telegraph will be working today, and perhaps only the Western Union—the Postal Telegraph will never hold up as well as the Western Union."

Betty Ann giggled. She had had her fun with Tod.

"That dog!" his father scoffed. "He'll go home all right. Just give him a little time. And stop worrying!"

Yet Tod could not help worrying until he knew his dog was safely home. As his father stepped outside, Tod realized that he had missed another opportunity to inquire whether his father had bought Gerry's new license.

Left alone with his sister, Tod wondered if maybe Betty Ann would tell him more about her fight with Mike, but she kept a stubborn silence. The shelves were soon covered, and Tod began to feel weariness from their long trek through the fire. Betty Ann seemed to be folding up, as she began to complain about the cold. When they had first entered the factory, coming in out of the chilly day, it had seemed warm. But this was only the heat left over from the day before, since the janitor did not come in on Sundays.

"Oh, well, it's better than being outdoors," Betty Ann grumbled. "Let's try to sleep." She pulled her father's chair up, put her muff on the desk, and laid her head wearily on it.

Tod brought up another chair, and sitting at the other end of the desk he crossed his arms and put his head down on them. He wished his father would hurry back. Then he could do *something* about Gerry, he wasn't sure exactly what, but he wanted to do *something*.

He dozed, but did not know whether he had slept a long time or only for a moment when he heard the outer door click open, and he looked up with relief. It was not their father, however, but a very stout, very dirty, and very unhappy-looking Western Union Telegraph messenger boy, known to almost everyone in the center of Baltimore as Teddy.

"Golly!" the boy said, closing the door and limping into the room. "I never figured I'd find you two here. I tried the door because I thought maybe your father had come down on account of the fire and that maybe he could help me."

"He'll be back soon, if you want him. What's wrong?" Tod said. "Teddy, you look as if you'd been in the fire."

"Don't call me Teddy when I'm wearing this uniform, Tod. It sounds too much like a Teddy bear. At Western Union, my name is Theodore Delgrad. But with any old name I had a fierce day of it." He eased himself into a chair, took off his Western Union cap and put it carefully on the table.

"Well, what happened, Mister Theodore Delgrad?" Tod teased.

"What happened? First I got soaked when one of those wornout hoses broke, then I got soot all over me when I got too close to the fire so I could see it,

71

and then—" He touched his ankle and grunted with pain.

"Then—well, it was just up the street, I fell over a pile of bricks, in the middle of the sidewalk. I hurt my ankle, maybe I sprained it. Anyhow I can hardly walk on it. I was headed for the Harford Road, when it happened."

"The Harford Road!" Tod said. "That's a long way out, Teddy." He didn't even attempt to call him Theodore Delgrad. He had never called him anything but Teddy.

"It hurts something fierce, and I can hardly stand on that foot," Teddy said.

"Maybe I could wrap it tight for you, T-T-Theodore, and it wouldn't hurt so much." Betty Ann began looking around for something to use as a bandage and finally took one of the pieces of canvas and tore it into strips.

"This won't look very pretty, but it's clean, and it will support your ankle."

"Who cares about looks if it helps?" Teddy said, and Betty Ann knelt and wrapped the ankle, while Teddy talked. "What a day! You can't go anywhere directly. You have to go all around where the fire is burning. I was trying to get to the Harford Road car when I fell. I'll never make it now, and I've got to let the office know. I just couldn't go any farther on this ankle, and then I remembered The Morton Shoe, and I thought maybe your father would be down here,

72

and maybe he could find someone to take the message back to the Western Union Office."

"Can you get home, then, Teddy? Do you live far away?" Betty Ann asked.

"Now that you've wrapped the ankle, I'm pretty sure I can get home. I live only five or six blocks away, and I'll manage somehow. It's the message I'm worried about."

"Tod will jump at a chance to get inside of a Western Union Office," Betty Ann laughed.

"Sure," Tod said eagerly, "I'll take it back. What branch office does it go to?"

"Everything is all mixed up, Tod." Teddy wiggled nervously. "The branch offices are all closed down, at least most of them are. You should see the newspaper reporters trying to send out their stories. Right smack in the middle of a sentence the wires go down. The only office we are sure of is the main office in the Equitable Building. At least that one is safe, because it is in a fireproof building.

"If it isn't delivered, this message has got to go back to the Western Union," Teddy said, in a discouraged voice. "Then they'll have to send it out again, all the way to Harford Road, and they don't have nearly enough messengers." He rubbed his eyes, already red from the smoke. "I'm in all sorts of trouble. I don't know *what* I should do."

Tod reached over and picked up Teddy's Western Union cap. It had seen a lot of wear and its outlines had lost their trimness. The dirt and smoke had not helped any, but it was still a badge of the Western Union. He put it on. Suddenly he felt capable of walking all the way across Baltimore, on his hands if necessary.

"Teddy, could I deliver the telegram for you?" he said.

"You! Well—" Teddy's face brightened as he considered. "Usually you couldn't—it would cost me my job. But right now I guess the only thing the Western Union cares about is getting its messages delivered."

The front door clicked open and Mr. Morton entered.

"Tell Father about it," Betty Ann said to Tod.

Tod did not make a very good job of it, and at the first mention of the Western Union, his father looked suspicious.

"Did you two boys fix this up between you?" Mr. Morton demanded.

"Fix?" Tod asked angrily. "Teddy can't walk any distance with that ankle. He's lucky if he can make it to his own house. You can see how it's swollen."

"Mr. Morton," Teddy protested, "I didn't even know that Tod was here. I came in because I couldn't go any farther and I hoped somehow that you could help me out."

"Maybe Tod could take it back to whatever office it came from," Mr. Morton said.

"Which office?" Teddy said. "The one it came

74

from was closing down as soon as it got out this batch of messages. It would have to go to the main office and in the meantime a lot of time would be lost."

"Well, I guess it's not so important that it can't wait a little. The only thing really important is getting this fire out," Mr. Morton said.

"That's just it, Mr. Morton." Teddy's pain and disappointment showed in his frown and in his pulling each finger—one after another in the intensity of his thought. "Did you know they are calling out the militia, both the Fourth and the Fifth Regiments?* By telephone, by telegraph, every way possible. This message is calling one of the reserves to report for duty. Of course I'm not supposed to tell what is in messages, but you see, Mr. Morton, it is important. You see why no time should be lost and why I'm willing to take a chance on letting Tod deliver this message. I guess, tonight, there aren't any rules. We just have to stop the fire." Teddy's forehead was wet with perspiration, and he seemed almost at the point of tears as he finished.

"I see, Teddy," Mr. Morton said humbly. "It's that bad, is it, that the militia is being called out?"

"Bad?" Teddy said. "There's only one office in Baltimore that we're sure of and that is the main office." He turned to Tod. "It isn't difficult to get out there, Tod. You take the Harford Road car at Balti-

---

* Naval Reserves and Army units from Fort McHenry were also called out.

more Street. It will be a long ride, about an hour. Then another hour to come back. Then you will have to report back to the main office."

"This means a great deal to you, doesn't it, Tod?" his father said.

"Oh, Dad." Never before had Tod spoken so freely to his father. "Just imagine being a Western Union operator right now."

"And what would you be doing?" his father smiled.

"I'd be telling the whole world, everywhere, 'BIG FIRE IN BALTIMORE.'"

"But Tod—" Teddy looked at him with a new respect, "that's just what they are doing."

"Is it all right, Dad, may I go?" Tod asked.

"Yes, I guess so. You will be helping to fight the fire too, if only in a small way. It seems the *right* thing to do. Get back home as fast as you can. Your mother will worry," he smiled, "and so will I."

"Can I wear your cap, Teddy?" Tod asked.

"Nope." Teddy grabbed his cap and held it firmly. "I don't dare let you wear it. After all you are not a *real* Western Union messenger."

Tod placed the message carefully in his inside coat pocket, together with the paper that must be signed by the person receiving the message. As he went toward the door, he heard his father say in an amused voice, "I guess Tod wished so hard for a Western Union telegram to deliver that it just *had* to come true."

"Wish?" Betty Ann laughed. "Didn't I hear something about Tod's fighting with you yesterday for the privilege of delivering messages instead of shoes?"

"Oh, well," Mr. Morton said good-naturedly, "when I was his age, I wanted to be a magician."

"But Mr. Morton," Teddy said, "Tod knows more about the Western Union than lots of the old operators, and he's always trying to learn more."

"To say nothing of that gate latch, that he bangs away on every day—" Betty Ann said.

The gate latch! His father was never home when he practiced. Tod was pretty sure that once he learned about it, he would consider it a big waste of time.

Tod closed the door quietly and slipped out into the black, smoke-laden night.

7

Tod had listened to Teddy's directions for getting to Harford Road, but he already knew the way. There was no problem if you took the right trolley car at Baltimore Street, for you just rode and rode and got off the car when you reached the right street number on Harford Road.

As he started walking north to Baltimore Street, he could see that the fire was spreading with awful speed. The Sun Building was in ruins. Buildings exploded and disintegrated into shapeless masses of brick and mortar, lighted by flaming brands. Everything seemed to be in flames. Rosin ran out of timbers and made rivers of fire. The wooden blocks that paved some of the downtown streets had caught fire, so that the entire center of each street blazed. Telegraph poles flared like enormous torches; whenever one of them collapsed, it brought down masses of glowing wires with it.

Fighting for breath, brushing off red-hot cinders, Tod finally reached Baltimore Street. There had been times when he thought he would never make it. As he stood waiting for the trolley car, a grim policeman approached him.

"You won't get a streetcar tonight, son," the policeman said. "They've all stopped running."

"Stopped running? But I must get to the Harford Road to deliver a message."

"No streetcars running anywhere in the city." The policeman shook his head. "If you want to get to Harford Road tonight, you'll just have to walk."

Walk? All the way to Harford Road? It was miles and miles. Yet his errand and the reason for it kept digging into his mind. He had a message to deliver—an important message.

A hot blast struck his back. It battered him like a great wind in a storm—a fire storm with the pulsing air full of fiery bits of debris. Bending his head, he began to walk.

He managed to turn a corner and get out of the burning gale. Only the roar of the fire came to him as he stood trying to get his breath back. Then a new sound came. The bell in the City Hall began to toll.

Dong-dong-dong—it rang three times and stopped. Then it continued and rang three times and paused, and again three times, dong-dong-dong, and a pause. The solemn tolling of the bell became almost as terrifying as the fire itself. The doleful sound seemed to be calling mourners to a tremendous funeral. Did they toll a bell when a city died?

"What's the bell for?" Tod asked a man rushing past him, but the man dashed away. He asked another man, and still another, but everyone seemed to be hurrying, and no one had time to answer him.

"What's the bell for?" Tod asked an old man who was having a hard time keeping up with the crowd.

"Disaster! Signal for assembly!" the old man shouted. "They're calling out the National Guard."

That was what Teddy had said. Evidently the members of the Fourth and Fifth Regiments knew this signal. The man to whom this telegram was going, Mr. Joseph Dokings—he must know it too. Relief flooded over Tod. Perhaps there was no need for him to take the telegram to Harford Road.

The bell continued to toll—dong-dong-dong, dong-dong-dong. It rang loud and clear and terrifying. Tod could hear it plainly, but he knew in his secret heart that it could not be heard miles away, far out on the Harford Road. Mr. Joseph Dokings would never know he was called up unless Tod could get the telegram to him. With a grim certainty Tod knew he must deliver the message.

People rushed past him. They all seemed to have gone mad. It was worse even than this afternoon in Clay St., for then he had been with his father and sister. He was all alone now and filled with terror.

As people yelled at him and pushed him, he told himself that he must not get so frightened, he must not lose his head, for this was the worst thing to do in a crowd. He must keep his mind on what he had to do—to get the message to Mr. Dokings.

The bell tolled, on and on, dong-dong-dong.

People seemed to be going toward the City Hall, or were they heading toward the Fifth Regiment Armory in response to the tolling bell?

Then, quite suddenly, everyone turned around and started in the opposite direction. Hysterical people pushed him and twisted him around and he was carried along with the crowd. He couldn't understand it. Why had the people turned and fled in the opposite direction? They tripped over his feet, and they almost knocked him down in their flight.

"Step along, boy!" someone yelled.

"Get out of the way! They're going to dynamite!"

"Hurry up, will you? Get going."

They seemed so violent that they frightened Tod.

A man carrying a child and a small suitcase paused long enough to say, "Hurry! Don't block the way! Do you want to get burned up? Run, kid, run!"

Another man repeated "Run," and the word went through the crowd of frightened people. Run! Run! And everyone was running. In panic, Tod ran, too. He did not know where he was going. He went with the crowd. Blindly, without reason or direction, he raced until his breath was gone. Then he stopped, sucked in tainted air, and ran again. A stabbing pain in his side made him realize he could run no farther.

He pushed himself against a stone wall, and clung to it as the frightened mob went past him. Looking up he saw the Washington Monument, and

knew he was somewhere near Mt. Vernon Place. He braced himself against the rough surface of the wall and looked back toward the fire.

No wonder everyone had run. Burning in the sky like a monstrous bonfire, the "fireproof" Equitable Building, the headquarters of the Western Union, the spot where Mike was at work, was exploding in billowing flames, up and up and up into the heavens.

Tod's knees buckled under him and he slid down until his exhausted body lay flat on the ground. He knew now that the last safety in Baltimore was gone. The center of the city was a furnace. Nothing could save it.

His eyelids drooped as his tortured gaze saw that against the smoke-filled sky, Baltimore was burning its heart out. Fatigue at last made his weary eyes close, as sleep overcame him.

8

Tod was sure he was having a nightmare, for in a world that was burning up, he was freezing to death. His head hit something hard, and he realized he had been sleeping against a stone wall. It was not a nightmare. It was all *real*, the fire, the burning of the store, the loss of Gerry, and the Equitable Building in flames.

It was dark, but no street lamps were lighted. Whether it was still Sunday or whether it was Monday morning, Tod did not know. He could see a clear blue-black sky, sprinkled with stars when the billowing pinkish clouds parted. To the north the Washington Monument was bathed in a rosy glow reflected from the sky. He was not sure how he had gotten here. He remembered being swept along with the crowd, then hanging on to the stone wall when he was too tired to go farther.

He sat up, but he felt so dizzy that he leaned back against the wall. His eyes stung with grit, and his throat was dry.

After a few minutes he got slowly to his feet. The telegram! He poked his fingers into the inside coat pocket and felt the envelope. He hadn't lost it, thank goodness!

He would deliver the message! And then what? He could not report delivery to the Superintendent of Messengers as he had hoped. There *was* no Superintendent of Messengers. There was no building left —neither the main office nor the branch offices. Maybe there was no Western Union.

He brushed a fragment of burning paper from his sleeve, and realized that he still had miles to go to get to the address on Harford Road.

He was tired and cold and hungry. Maybe he should just give up and go home. Nobody would care, perhaps nobody would even know, if he failed to deliver the message. Surely no one would blame him.

Unless he blamed himself.

The message, Teddy had said, was to one of the militia men, calling him out to join his regiment, to help control the crowds during the fire. This was certainly as important a job as the policemen and firemen had.

He watched all these men in uniform now with a new understanding. He wondered how long they had been on duty. Their figures stood out black against the weird red glow toward the south. They stood there, solid and steady, directing people and keeping them from going toward the fire.

Maybe Baltimore was doomed, but its people would never give up, Tod thought. They were like his father, who had resolved to open a new store as he stared at the ruins of the old. They were like Sales, opening the safe and loading valuables into the baby buggy, while walls threatened to explode; and yes, like his sister Betty Ann, staying bravely with her father—knocking off his hat to beat out an ember with her cherished beaver muff. Teddy, too, fourteen years old, with a sprained ankle, had never given up until he had entrusted his message to Tod to deliver.

Mike? Was he safe? What had happened to him when the Western Union took fire? Tod was very sure that Mike would stay at his key until the last minute.

He, Tod Morton, must be like this, too.

He turned his face toward the northeast and the Harford Road. He tried to walk fast but he had a feeling that all his bones were broken. He had always thought how wonderful it would be to deliver messages; not shoes, but messages. At last his chance had come, but he had never imagined anything like this.

He turned his back on the fire, and knew he was going in the right direction when he saw the elevated tracks at Guilford Avenue looming ahead of him. Walking into the shadows made by the elevated, he heard a groan, and a mumble. Looking harder, he discovered, behind a huge concrete pillar, a feeble old man trying to get a cart out of a rut in the cobblestones.

Tod went closer and peered into a wrinkled old face full of despair. Then he took hold of the cart handle, and gave a tug. At first it would not budge, but when they both gave a good shove, the cart rolled free. Tod ducked when the old man burst out in a volley of foreign words and tried to embrace him. He gathered that the man wanted to be taken somewhere and there was no use trying to explain that he couldn't help. Yet Tod didn't want to walk off and leave him. Then he saw some people walking toward them, pushing their possessions in a cart. Tod called to them and a boy about his own age came over.

"I don't know what the old man is saying," Tod explained unhappily to the other boy, while a flood of words poured around them. "Can you understand him?"

"He's speaking Russian," the boy said. "I'm Polish, and I get a little of it. He says he wants to go to a sister in Walbrook. We'll take him along with us."

"Where are you going?"

"To Forest Park, to our uncle's. We'll drop the old man at Walbrook. He's from East Baltimore like us. The whole section will go once the fire jumps Jones' Falls, so everybody is heading for the country."

"If the fire goes east, our factory will be right in its path," Tod said. "It's the Morton Shoe Factory."

"Oh," the boy said. "Yes, yes, we know The Morton Shoe." He seemed to hesitate and then said gently, "If the fire goes east, your factory will probably go even before the fire jumps Jones' Falls."

"Yes," Tod said. The boys looked at each other silently for a moment. Then the Polish boy said, "You just ought to see the people in East Baltimore. The old folks are half-crazy, and you can't blame them. My grandparents spent years in trying to get to this country and make a new home. Now they are afraid everything's going to burn down. Maybe it will. Maybe a lot of people won't have a roof over their heads in the morning."

It was bad enough for stores and buildings and shops going up in flames, but Tod could not bear to think of homes being burned, too.

"They say that if the wind keeps shifting around," he heard the other boy say, "it may save East Baltimore, but then there's a chance that it will reach the homes in West Baltimore."

If it went west, it could strike the Mortons' home. Then they'd be homeless, Tod thought. Maybe with all their belongings in a pushcart. He looked toward the west. Should he give up trying to deliver the message and go home? He touched the yellow envelope in his pocket.

"Goodbye," he called over his shoulder as he turned and ran. "Take care of yourselves and the old man." He sprinted as fast as he could in the direction of Harford Road.

Out of breath, he came to the group of buildings that was the Maryland Penitentiary. He halted and looked at the hooded windows that rose in overhang-

ing, rounded arches near the roof. They always reminded him of watching eyes. He turned away.

When he reached Greenmount Avenue, he came
to the old Greenmount Cemetery. Walking along the
sidewalk, he saw a boy looking toward the fire. He
could not believe his eyes. Yet tonight he guessed
anything might happen, for the boy was surely Ham,
but a Ham dressed like other boys, in overcoat and
cap.

"Hey!" Tod cried.

"Hey!" Ham whirled around. "What do you
know? It's Tod Morton."

They stared at each other.

"What are you doing away out here?" Tod asked.

"What are you doing, yourself?" Ham asked in
a fighting voice.

"I'm delivering a Western Union message," Tod
told him, hoping that Ham realized how important
that was. "How did you get away over here in North
Baltimore?"

"My folks sent me to stay with my grandmother
out on York Road. They told me I had to take care
of her, but they don't fool me! They said that to keep
me from going to the fire! I sneaked out to get a look.
Were you down in the fire, Tod? Did you see whether
all those big buildings burned?"

"The Equitable Building is gone," Tod said.

"That building couldn't burn!" Ham was yelling
now. "It's fireproof."

"Well, it's gone, fireproof or not," Tod said. As

usual he and Ham were arguing. He couldn't remember a time when they were together that they hadn't quarreled.

"I'd like to see what's happening," Ham said, quite humbly for him. "Debbie went to the fire and so did you. Everybody went but me. It's not fair."

"A fire isn't a show," Tod said in a superior way, thinking of all he had gone through. "People are supposed to stay away from it unless they have business there."

"And I suppose you had business there," Ham sneered.

"Well, I did," Tod said. "I tried to help my father save the store. We were too late, though."

"The store? You mean it burned down?" Ham cried. Then his face changed, and his voice was low and sincere as he said, "That's too bad, Tod."

There was a stirring in the hedge that grew between the Cemetery and the sidewalk. Stark in winter nakedness, the shrubbery was nevertheless thick and gloomy, and the reflection from the red sky only made the denseness more mysterious.

Tod walked over to where there was a great lashing and waving of the bushes, and peered into their shadows.

"Watch out," Ham cringed away from the hedge and Tod saw that he was really frightened. "You remember that old John Wilkes Booth, the man who shot President Lincoln, is buried here. The teacher said that it's a secret just exactly where he is buried."

91

"Aw, we're not even inside the Cemetery," Tod said, following the disturbance in the bushes and trying to part the dead twigs.

"It might be the ghost of John Wilkes Booth," Ham said in a small scared voice.

"So you think his ghost wouldn't know where the Cemetery ends?" Tod jeered.

"Well, I just wish I had my lasso here, so I could protect us both," Ham said shakily.

"Protect us from what? You think you can lasso a ghost?" Tod began to laugh and pushed farther into the bushes where they quivered wildly. Then he stuck his hand down into the mass of shrubbery, and caught a little black hand, and looked into the face of a tiny black boy, so small he looked hardly able to walk; but there he was!

Tod pulled him from the hedge. The frightened child seemed ready to cry, so Tod leaned down and hugged him close, saying reassuring words all the time. In spite of this the boy began to whimper.

Ham came over, leaned down and put out a tentative finger and touched the child.

"Don't cry, little fellow," he said. "Don't cry. Look, I'll show you how I can whistle, shall I?"

The boy looked at Ham with big eyes and forgot to cry. Tod watched in amazement. He didn't know that Ham could whistle in any special way, but then he didn't know that Ham could do anything except use his lasso.

"Now you get ready," Ham said, "because it's

going to be a great big whistle. Ready?" and Ham let out a whistle that made more noise than a locomotive.

The child gurgled with laughter, and showed the beginnings of two white front teeth, as he patted his hands together in ecstasy.

Ham's whistle had another effect. A woman came running from across the street. She swooped down, and caught up the child in her arms.

"I've been looking all over for you, honey. How on earth did you get out?" She cuddled the boy in her arms. "He just loves to get over here where there are trees and bushes, even in the dark," she explained, as she patted the boy in her arms. Then she turned to ask Tod, "What do you hear about the fire? Will it come this far?"

"Maybe not," Tod said. "Up to now it's only the business section that has burned."

"That's what we heard. Usually the homes of us colored folks go first in any fire, but we haven't heard of anyone's home burning down." She seemed reassured, and with the baby in her arms she went back the way she had come.

The two boys continued northward on Greenmount Avenue. Trees overshadowed the street, making it dark and eerie, and the wind groaned through the dead branches.

"Now, if I just had my lasso," Ham said, and it occurred to Tod that Ham did not know where his lasso was.

"I'll give you back your old lasso," Tod promised. "It's in our cellar, but don't you ever try to lasso Gerry again." All Tod's anger at Ham welled up within him. "You lassoed him, and he ran away. He's lost and we don't know where he is."

"He's lost? But I—I—" Ham gulped. "But Gerry wouldn't stay away from you, Tod."

"He got locked in the store. It was Sales who got him out before the fire struck. But he's gone—gone, and there's a big fire raging, and he's lost again, and it's all your fault." Tod stopped because his voice was beginning to break, and he didn't want Ham to see him cry.

"Gee, Tod! He's lost? Gee. He's really *lost*."

Tod told him about Gerry's streaking out of the store when Sales opened the door to the back room, and that they had not seen him since. They hoped he had gone home.

"Poor Gerry!" Tod continued. "After being lassoed on Saturday afternoon, and locked in the store Saturday night, and caught in the fire on Sunday, Gerry probably doesn't know where he's safe. And *you*!" Tod's bitterness poured out. "You have to pretend you're a roaring cowboy, going around lassoing poor dumb beasts like Gerry—and kids, too—"

"I do that to scare people, and dogs, too, so they won't pick on me," Ham said in a small voice. "I wouldn't really hurt old Gerry."

"Wouldn't hurt him?" It was Tod who was yelling now. "How do you think it felt to have his legs pulled from under him and to be slammed down in the gutter?"

"Gee—I—I—" Ham didn't seem able to go on.

"Gerry could be a good friend to you," Tod said.

"Aw—w, who're you foolin'?" Ham said.

"He wants to play with you, doesn't he? That is, he did up until the time you lassoed him," Tod said.

"Well, I guess, yes, he always wants to play with me," Ham said in a surprised way, as if he had just discovered this.

"What would you have done to that tiny kid we found if you had had your lasso with you?" Tod said curiously.

"I'd have lassoed him, of course," Ham said.

"And scared him to death, and made his mother angry, and piled up a few more enemies—"

"But I have to protect myself. That kid was so little, of course I knew he wouldn't hurt me, and then you were here too. You see, I'm afr—" He stopped quickly before he said the word, but Tod knew. He knew now that Ham was afraid of people, afraid of dogs, afraid of many things.

They walked along in silence. Tod realized that he had never before talked this way with Ham. They had always been too busy arguing and yelling at each other.

"Anyhow," Tod said, "I'm glad you didn't have that old lasso with you tonight."

"Well," Ham's words came out slowly, "It seems funny to be without it."

They had reached North Avenue.

"He was a cute little kid, wasn't he?" Ham said. "He liked my whistle."

They lingered on the corner. It was here that Ham would go north and Tod would turn east on North Avenue. It came over Tod that for the last few minutes he had really enjoyed Ham's company, and he wished they could go farther together.

"Look, Tod," Ham said. "Tomorrow, just as soon as I get home, I'll help you hunt for Gerry. Don't worry. We'll find him." And Ham turned to cross the street as they both said goodbye.

9

Tod walked on with only his gloomy thoughts for
company. Suppose, just suppose that after he delivered his message and got home, just suppose that
Gerry was not there. Or suppose, just suppose that
his family had fled and there was *no one* there. Or
worse still, suppose that his home had already been
burned down.

To chase these awful thoughts, he tried to think
of how good it would be to find Mr. Joseph Dokings,
and to deliver his message. How very glad the
whole Dokings family would be that he had been
called to help the people of Baltimore in this terrible
fire.

No doubt the Dokings family would be so happy
that Tod had brought this message that they would
offer him a cookie or maybe a piece of cake. They
might even offer him a *nickle*.

Thinking of all the good things that would happen, he was surprised to find that he had reached the
Harford Road. His task now became more difficult,
because he would have to find the house number he

wanted. The houses were scattered, like homes in the country, and sometimes no number at all appeared on the gates that opened into big gardens.

Finally, by the light of the reflection from the red sky, he made out what he thought to be the number he was hunting. The house was a big black shadow that sat well back from the road. No light showed anywhere in the house.

He was leaning down to look more closely at the number on the gate, when he suddenly saw an old-fashioned lantern swinging down the road toward him. He waited until the man with the lantern came closer.

"Hey mister," Tod said and the lantern stopped.

"Who is it?" said the man carrying the lantern.

"Western Union," Tod announced loud and clear, and it sounded just the way he had always dreamed it would.

"*Western Union?*" the man gasped as if he didn't believe it.

"I have a telegram for Mr. Joseph Dokings—" Tod said.

"Good grief! It isn't his wife, is it? I mean—is somebody dead? His wife is visiting her folks in Pennsylvania. What is it, kid? Is it a death? How did you get out here? The street cars stopped running, didn't they?" the man hurled one question after another at Tod.

"Well, it isn't a death—but I'm not supposed to tell what is in telegrams," Tod said. "Anyhow it's a city message. But Mister, is Mr. Dokings at home, do you think? The house looks all dark."

"Well, of course, kid. All the houses are dark—it's late at night. A few people are staying up, though, because of the fire. I'm on my way to North Avenue to see if any of the stores are open. We need coal oil or we won't have any light. Maybe I can buy some candles too. No, Joe ain't there, he's down at the barn. Do you want me to take the telegram? I'll see him. It may be tomorrow before I do, but I'll see him."

Tomorrow? But Mr. Dokings was supposed to report *immediately*.

"The barn? You say Mr. Dokings is at the barn?" Tod asked.

"That's right," the man said. "We live next door and he passed our house about an hour ago. Said he was going down to help his farmer with a sick cow. He'll probably be there awhile."

"Is the barn far?" Tod asked.

"Far? No, it's not so far—that is, if you cut across fields. But you ain't plannin' to try to go there, are you?"

"I have to deliver this message to Mr. Joseph Dokings. Could you tell me how to get to the barn?"

"*Tonight?*" the man said. "Look, kid, I'll take the telegram. It can't be too important if it ain't a death and it ain't from his wife—I'll take it."

"It is important," Tod explained patiently. "I have to see that he gets it. Can you tell me how to get to the barn?"

"Well, sure. You just go down this road a piece and then you turn left on the second path—the second, not the first. Then you go down that path and you keep on going. It's quite a little way. You pass a small graveyard—just a little one—it's a family burying plot. After you pass it, you're almost there. You can't miss it. The path goes straight to it."

Tod repeated the directions carefully. He thanked the man and started down the road. He was so tired! He had thought when he reached Mr. Dokings' home that he had come to the end of his journey. Now, with still more ground to cover to get to the barn, he was almost overcome by his tiredness. His legs ached, and he longed to sit down, if only for a moment. Not only that, but he was starved, and he wanted a drink of water more than anything in the world.

There were no lights anywhere—not on the road, nor in any of the few houses that he passed. He came to the first path and watched carefully for the second. He was so long in coming to it that he wondered if he had missed it. Finally he reached a broad well-traveled path, and turned into it.

There were only wide, open fields on both sides of the path, and after leaving the Harford Road, he saw neither houses nor farm buildings. He heard no sound of horses or cows, either, and it was so lonesome that he would have welcomed even the squeal of a pig.

Ahead of him was a grove of trees, and the path

led straight into it. He was slowed down now because he could hardly see where he was going, except where a space in the overhanging trees allowed a ray of light from the fire-reddened sky to filter through. He came to a fence with a sturdy gate, and found the wooden peg that fastened it. It creaked open on rusty hinges. He had to struggle to close it, and the latch was so hard to refasten that he wished he had just climbed the fence—it would have been so much easier!

He went slowly, scarcely able to see his way. Then he stumbled, and when he tried to catch himself he slid on something hard that was wet and slippery. He peered down at a whitish, wide, flat stone, certainly not the kind of a thing that was usually found in the middle of a country path. He leaned over, and then put his fingers into what looked like carved letters, and he knew he was looking at a fallen tombstone, flat on the ground, surrounded by dirt and weeds.

At this moment he became conscious of whitish things all around him. They were surely gravestones, and this evidently was the old family burying ground. The man had not told him he would have to go *through* the cemetery.

Well, he told himself, he wasn't afraid of a few old tombstones, and he didn't believe in ghosts. Hadn't he made fun of Ham for being afraid when they walked past the Greenmount Cemetery?

He watched the path carefully, but in spite of

this he tripped on a tangled root. His head grazed an old tombstone and he sprawled face down. He got up a bit groggily.

He gulped as he saw a tall white figure to his right, with the head nodding as if to say, "No-no!" He closed his eyes tight, and then opened them quickly. The thing was still there, its head moving from side to side.

He didn't believe in ghosts, but his teeth chattered.

He leaned down and felt around for a rock. He picked one up, and taking a good aim, he flung it with all his might at the thing. He heard it smack. But what happened then was even worse than the nodding head, for the head fell off and went rolling among the tombstones.

Tod tottered on wobbling legs to a nearby stone and clung to it to hold himself up.

The head bounced around among the graves, and then uttered an unearthly "Yee—ow!" Tod began to laugh, at first shakily, and then loudly, as he realized that what he had seen was a cat, a big white pussycat who had evidently been sitting on the top of a tombstone.

His eyes had become accustomed to the gloom and he followed the path more easily now. The graveyard was small, and ahead of him the trees thinned out, and then were no more.

An open field stretched before him with a path that led directly to a barn. He came closer, and suddenly he saw a door open into the lighted barn, and then close again. This must be where he would find Mr. Joseph Dokings. He started to run, and surprised himself by being able to get some speed into his tired legs.

He reached the door. It opened easily, and by the light of a lantern, he saw two men bending over something in the straw. All he could think of was Gerry. Hurt? Dead? At the same time he knew perfectly well that it must be the sick cow lying there.

The younger man, wearing a heavy coat, a knitted cap and muddy rubber boots, must be Mr. Joseph Dokings. The older man must have dressed out of the pickings of a rag bag, from the old cap with a frayed peak, to the worn brown leggings, held together with string where the buttons were missing.

The two men, startled at hearing him, turned their heads.

"Look, Joe," the older man said.

"Yeah—" Joe said. They both stared at Tod.

Tod let go of the door and tried to pull out the telegram quickly, but it was stuck. When he finally got it out, it was sadly crumpled.

"Western Union," he said. "Telegram for Mr. Joseph Dokings," and he handed it to the younger man.

"Well—uh—uh—for *me*? Away out here?" Joseph Dokings looked at the telegram and then at Tod. "How on earth—"

"Watch it, Joe," the older man called in alarm, "Joe—hold her! She's trying to get up."

Joe stuffed the telegram in his pocket and turned back to the cow. Both men gave all their attention to her. Tod waited a moment and then said, "Mr. Dokings, you have to sign for it—that you received it, you know."

The cow groaned and grumbled, a mournful mooing sound. The two men were very busy with her.

"What? What did you say, kid? Wait a minute. I'll be with you," Mr. Dokings called out.

It seemed to Tod that the cow must be terribly sick. He saw now that the farmer was sitting on the cow's head. Tod walked over to a small stool and sat down gratefully, prepared to wait, and glad to rest his tired feet.

He hadn't realized how tired he was, for suddenly he was half asleep, still hearing the most agonizing cries of the animal; and all he could think of was Gerry! His dog was being burned to death—no, he was caught under the thundering hoofs of the fire horses—Gerry lost and forsaken—no, yelping in pain right here in the barn with him. Tod, fighting his way up out of the depths of slumber, jumped up from the stool. Then he realized it was the cow! His heart still pounded with fright, and he started toward the door. He had never heard such pitiful screams from an animal. He would go outside and wait.

Then Mr. Dokings came toward him, holding the open telegram in his hand.

"Where do I sign?" he said. "Gosh, this telegram says to report for duty immediately. Fire must be spreading! Well, anyhow, it doesn't mean a death in the family like telegrams usually do." He smiled good-naturedly, and took the paper and pencil that Tod held out to him. Then, handing them back, he seemed to consider Tod seriously for the first time.

"Say, son, how did you get out here? Somebody said the streetcars had all stopped running," he said.

"I walked."

"You walked!" Joe went speechless for a moment. "*You walked!*" he said at last. "Well now, look, you can't walk all the way back. It's too far," he said.

"Joe! *Joe!* I think she's dying!" the farmer yelled.

Joe rushed back to the cow.

"Aw—ww!" Joe examined the cow and then said, "She's all right if you just get up off her head." Then Joe yelled to Tod over the cow's bellowings, "Look, son, curl up in that straw and go to sleep. I'll have to go to the city and we'll find some way to get a ride. If it's the cow that's bothering you, she'll stop bellowing soon. It was just something she ate, nothing serious!"

Nothing serious! The cow thrashed around in the straw. All Tod wanted was to get away, far away from the barn where the piteous animal lay, for he could not stand the heartbreaking cries.

"Thank you, sir," Tod said, "I can't wait. My family will be worried about me, and I have to report delivery of my message."

He hurried away from the barn. He might not make any better time than if he had waited until morning when he could have gotten a ride back. At least he was on his way, and he would not be reminded every minute that his Gerry had been in the fire and was not yet accounted for.

Tod went back through the grove of trees, and at the entrance to the little graveyard the big white cat met him. She meeowed in a friendly way and rubbed against his leg, and she went with him all the way through the cemetery.

10

Tod had been so glad to get away from the barn, and the poor suffering cow, that he had forgotten how hungry he was, and how thirsty. He doubted, however, that there had been any drinking water in the barn, for the two buckets-full that he had seen were surely never intended for drinking purposes.

He had delivered his message, and now what? Where could he report delivery? Teddy had said that the branch office from which the message had come had been burned out and that all the offices were closing. He had hoped to rush into the office—messenger boys always rushed—and pull out the signature of Joseph Dokings and show it to the Superintendent of Messengers, who would be so impressed that he would promise him a job next summer. But now, there was no Superintendent of Messengers, there was no office, maybe there was no Western Union.

He put his hand into his pocket and touched the paper with the signature of Joseph Dokings, but he had no idea what to do with it. Finally he decided grudgingly that it was useless to try to find the

Western Union in the middle of the night, so he would go home and hunt for it the first thing in the morning.

He reached North Avenue and turned toward the west. He groaned as he thought of the long walk home. Whenever he had to go from East Baltimore to West Baltimore the distance seemed twice as far as it really was.

His thirst grew worse and worse. If he could see a house that was brightly lighted, and where people seemed to be awake, he would go and ask for a drink of water. In some of the homes along North Avenue, a gas jet burned in the hall, but there was no sign of anyone being up and around. The rows of houses sat silent and forbidding.

His feet hurt, and he wished he could take off his shoes, but his feet were so badly swollen that he feared he would never get them on again. They were his best shoes—or they had been until this morning. Now, they were wrecked beyond repair.

He stopped at a corner and leaned against a lamp post. He held up first one foot and then the other, trying to rest them, but he couldn't tell whether this helped or not. His tongue felt twice its size and he kept thinking—if only he could get a drink.

Then he saw it! He couldn't believe his eyes! A drinking fountain, an old-fashioned lion's head, grinned at him from the corner wall of a building.

Tod knew it was one of the few left in the city, for they were fast disappearing. That there should be one here and now, when he needed it, was almost too good to be true.

As he ran toward it, he knew there was something, *something* not quite right about it.

His hand groped automatically for the iron drinking-cup that was always chained to these fountains. It wasn't there. He raised his eyes to the stone lion's head, and saw with despair what was missing. No water gushed from the mouth of the lion. Desperately he banged it, and then tried to shake the old lion's head. Frantically he hammered it with his fists. Not even a trickle of water came out. Evidently the water had been turned off but the fountain had not yet been removed.

He sagged against the fountain, too despondent for tears. He'd never get home. He'd never get to the Western Union. He wondered how long it took a person to die of thirst.

He didn't know how long he stood there, letting the fountain hold him up. He kept thinking that maybe, just maybe, the water would suddenly gush forth. He could not believe that no water would ever again come from the lion's mouth.

Finally he heaved a deep sigh and pulled himself erect. He faced toward the west, and with a determined effort he started to walk.

Then he remembered the North Avenue Station,

for the Maryland and Pennsylvania Railroad* was on his route home. It was such a small station that he doubted that it would be open all night, but for a moment he walked a little faster, thinking how good a drink of water would be.

He had gone several blocks when he heard a wagon rattling behind him and coming closer. The horse's hoofs, clopping along the quiet streets, seemed very loud. The wagon caught up with him, drew to the curb and stopped. A man and a woman, both on the seat of a spring wagon, leaned forward.

"Hello there!" the man said. "Do you want a lift?"

Tod's mouth was so dry that he nodded and tried to say, "Yes, please."

He saw that they were colored people and very old. He wondered what they were doing on the street on this terrible night, as the woman reached down a hand to help him climb over the wheel.

"We didn't know the fire was so bad," the woman said, her voice low and sad. "We came in like we always do, to bring our butter and eggs to Lexington Market. We got our crates in the back of the wagon, taking them all home again. We heard there was a fire, but we didn't figure on anything like this. It looks awful!"

"How come you're out in it?" the man said.

---

* The Maryland and Pennsylvania Railroad, known as the "Ma and Pa," is no longer in existence.

"I—I—live—West Baltimore," Tod managed to croak. He pointed to his mouth. "Too dry—can't talk."

"Why, you poor boy," exclaimed the woman. "Jack, get that jug of water in the back there."

The man reached down and hoisted it out. He poured while the woman held the cup.

"Take it slow, boy," the man warned. Tod took a sip and held it in his mouth, then another and another. He had never tasted anything so good.

"You're covered with soot," the woman said. "Were you in the fire?"

Tod nodded. Then, refreshed by the drink of water, he told them about the store burning down, and the message that he had delivered. He told them where he lived, and they said of course they would drive him home.

Tod sat between the man and woman trying to keep awake, but right in the middle of a sentence his head jerked forward and he almost fell off the seat. Gently the woman pulled him over against her shoulder. He saw, however, that they had left North Avenue, and realized in a sleepy sort of way that they were trying for a cross-street farther to the south. He dozed and woke and dozed again. The monotonous drone of the rolling wagon wheels lulled him into an uneasy sleep. Then he suddenly came wide-awake as the wagon jolted to an abrupt halt, and they were confronted by several policemen and firemen.

"Where are you going?" One of the policemen asked, in a tired voice that had the firmness of authority.

"Home. If we ever get there," the old man replied.

"But why are you going toward the fire?" Policemen and firemen gathered around.

One of the firemen carried an old-fashioned lantern that gave little more light than came from the reddened sky. Tod could see that their tired faces were smeared with soot, and that their uniforms looked as if they had been worn every day for months.

"We're going toward Carrollton Avenue," the old man explained patiently. "That's where the boy lives, and then we'll go on home to Pikesville."

"Oh, sure," one of the firemen spoke with relief in his voice. "I know you. You have a stall in Lexington Market, don't you? Who's the boy?"

"I'm Tod Morton, sir," Tod answered. "I was downtown with my father. We lost the store but my father thinks the fire will not reach the factory. But then—I—well, I had to deliver a message for the Western Union, out on Harford Road."

"But there are no cars running—" a fireman interrupted.

"No. I had to walk."

"*You walked!* To Harford Road!" the fireman said, and Tod realized that he didn't believe this was possible.

"Yes, sir, and the man signed for it." Tod brought out the paper. "Then, on North Avenue, these nice people picked me up and said they would take me home."

"The Harford Road! What do you think of that!" the fireman said to the other firemen standing around the wagon. He handed the paper back to Tod and there was respect in his voice as he gave directions. "Now look: Don't go south any farther. Turn west at the next corner and you will be all right, I think. Of course we don't know what may happen, so keep going, and go fast!" He waved them on.

The old man said "Giddap!" and then talked to the horse in a sing-song of meaningless words. The horse broke into a burst of speed, smooth and steady, and Tod slumbered once more.

When he awoke again, he was being carried up his own front steps as if he were sick or something. He squirmed from the old man's arms and got to his feet as they entered the vestibule.

Betty Ann and Cora were in the hall and they both looked at him wide-eyed with amazement. His sister's face was very white and Cora's hair was straggling down from her Psyche knot.

"Oh, Tod dear," Betty Ann said. "Are you hurt?" And she gave him a big hug.

"Oh, I'm fine!" Tod said. "These folks picked me up when I was so tired I didn't know if I could take another step."

Cora was speechless with surprise for a moment,

then went to the old woman and invited her and her husband to have coffee and cake, and they all moved toward the kitchen.

Tod made straight for the icebox, and was soon wolfing down cold roast beef as he stood at the kitchen sink, talking between bites.

"I delivered that Western Union message," he said proudly to Betty Ann. "Tell Mike, that is—do you know where he is?"

"Mike! We *don't* know where he is!" she said with a catch in her voice. "The Equitable Building is gone—"

So Betty Ann knew about the loss of the main office. No wonder she looked so white and scared.

"But where's Mother?" Tod said. "Did she go to bed?" He was disappointed, for Mrs. Morton never went to bed before everyone was home.

"Mother. Oh, Tod!" Betty Ann began to cry.

Tod's heart sank down and down. His mother! What on earth had happened to her? Something awful or she would have been at the door to meet him.

"What—what happened?" he managed to say.

"We don't know, Tod." Betty Ann was crying so hard he could hardly understand her. "Tod, she never came home! She went down to see if Aunt Matilda needed her. She thought maybe Aunt Matilda and Uncle Will would have to leave their house and come up here. They are near the center of the city. But Tod, that was early yesterday evening."

"Well, of course, she would have to walk home—" Tod said.

"But Tod, Biddle Street is not so far, and it is almost dawn. Oh, Tod."

"Sh-hh, don't cry so hard, Betty Ann. Won't we wake Dad?" Tod said. "He got home all right, didn't he?"

"He's still at the factory," Betty Ann said, as she wiped her eyes. "But Sales is with him. That boy, sick as he was, came back to help in any way he could. So Dad sent me home with the most important things in the safe—as much as I could carry. I think Dad will be all right. But Mother—she told Cora she would come home as soon as she was sure Aunt Matilda didn't need her."

They looked at each other in bewilderment. Their mother never left the house without telling them when she expected to get back. Of course she would want to help her sister Matilda and her husband, but the fire had not come to Biddle Street. At least Tod thought it had not because the firemen on the street had seemed to think it would go to the east, not the north. Then why hadn't his mother come home? Why hadn't she brought Aunt Matilda and Uncle Will back with her? Surely something terrible had happened.

The two old people ate but little of Cora's best cake and cookies, but they drank several cups of coffee. They were nervous and anxious to go on their way. Before they left, Cora invested some of the household money in a quantity of butter and eggs from the back of their wagon. They finally departed for their home in Pikesville.

As soon as they had gone, Tod looked at Cora. "Gerry?" he said, but he knew that if the dog had come home, he would have been at the door to welcome him.

"We looked everywhere," Cora said sadly. "I looked and your mother looked too before she went to Aunt Matilda's. Then after she went, I kept going to the door and calling him every little while." She looked at him anxiously as she said, "Tod, honey, did you get enough to eat? You poor kid, are you still thirsty?"

"Yes, I am, Cora," Tod said, "and I don't think I'll ever get enough water as long as I live."

He started to say goodnight and then remembered that neither his father nor his mother was at home.

"Cora, can I help close up?" he said.

"No, Tod, thank you. Everything is locked and bolted, so you just go on to bed," Cora said.

"The roof, Betty Ann," he exclaimed, as they started up the steps. "Maybe I'd better get up there and be ready to put out any sparks that come over."

"It isn't necessary, Brother." She called him "brother" only when she liked him a lot. She continued as she followed him into his room. "We all thought our roofs were safe, because they are of tin. But Cora says that Mrs. Strickler's grape arbor caught fire from a flying ember. The neighbors put it out before it reached the house, but now there are several men in the block taking turns watching the roofs.

"I'll get you another blanket," she said. She certainly was treating him well. While she was gone, he got into his night clothes and snuggled in between the sheets, thinking that he would tell her about meeting Ham, and about the ghost and the cow.

Betty Ann came back with the blanket and spread it on top of the others. Then she sat down on the side of the bed, and he saw that she was anxious to talk about something important.

"Tod, did I tell you?" She spoke in a whisper. "We—ll, Mike and I had a fight."

"Yes, that's what you said." He was glad she was going to tell him about it. "What on earth could you find to fight about with Mike?"

"I wanted—I wanted him to take me to Sally's house, tonight. She was having a few couples in. But Mike had to work. You know, Brother, that Western Union operators never have any Sundays or holidays off. Of course, they get passes for all the shows, but even so, they can't always get time off to use them. Once in a while they take a day off, but they are never *sure*, so that they can make a hard-and-fast *date*. Now, Brother, how can a girl have any fun at all if she never knows if her fellow can take her someplace? So we had a fight. And oh, Tod, maybe he's dead. Maybe he died for that old Western Union."

"Gee!" Tod sat up in bed and put his arm around her.

"Do you think he's safe?" she said. "Do you think he got out of the Equitable Building in time?"

"Gee!" He remembered the Equitable Building as he had last seen it, with the flames devouring it.

"This awful fire!" she continued. "And that isn't the worst of it. Because of the fire, Sally didn't have her party. Oh, Tod." Betty Ann dabbed her eyes and suddenly, without warning, she was sobbing on his shoulder. It scared him, because Betty Ann *never* cried, well, hardly ever. His arm tightened around her and he felt a million years older than his sister. She was the one who was always talking about a man doing his duty. Mike was doing a very important job, and maybe the fire had made her realize that it was also a very dangerous job. Maybe she would never see him again.

Tod wanted to comfort her, but what could he say? For everything was being consumed in this burning city. In a few hours, the fire might be at their door. He tried to say tomething to reassure her, but he had seen too much to be very hopeful. Moreover, he well knew that Mike would stay at his key at the Western Union as long as possible.

What about his father? Tod hoped he was safe. At least he had Sales with him. His mother—where was she? It was not like her to stay out all night; why hadn't she let the family know anything at all? And Gerry! Poor Gerry, wandering around in the fire, unable to find his way home, or maybe tied up some-where, and crying his heart out—or else maybe *dead*.

Tod found that his cheeks were wet, and they were *his* tears. He wiped them away with the back of his hand. He held Betty Ann closer and a great surge of affection came over him. She was home and she was *safe*. And after all, as a sister Betty Ann was just about as good as they came.

"Tell you what!" he said, trying to be cheerful. He had no idea what he could tell her, but when Betty Ann looked at him so expectantly through her tear-brimmed eyes, he knew he must say *something*. "Well—well—now let's make our plans so we know where to start in the morning. Now, first we find Mother. Right?"

"Yes, oh, yes." Betty Ann said.

"Then—then—well, maybe Gerry will come home by that time—" it made him feel better to say it, even if he did not really believe it. "So then we go down-town to the factory. If everything is all right there, and Sales is there to help, and Dad does not need us, then we go to the Western Union." He finished with so much hope in his voice that Betty Ann was almost cheerful.

"Oh, Tod, that's what we'll do. You're wonderful. You always come up with some sort of an idea." She gave him a quick kiss, turned out the gas, and walked out with a light step.

He hadn't been able to tell her anything about his own troubles getting to the Harford Road, or about the delivery of the message, not yet reported to the Western Union.

He was so worried that he thought he would not sleep at all. He snuggled down in the cool white sheets, and thought how strange it was that he had never before noticed how comfortable his own bed was, and how downy the pillows. So much better than where he had spent last night, sleeping against a stone wall on Mt. Vernon Place.

11

Tod was sure he had just gone to sleep, when the small noises of people stirring brought him awake on Monday morning. He opened one eye and saw that it was broad daylight.

He heard the door open, and his mother looked in.

"Mother!" he yelled.

She came over to the bed and put her arms around him and held him very tight. She still wore her outdoor dress of dark plum color, so he knew she had just come home.

"But Mother! Where have you been? What happened?"

"Now, where do you think?" she smiled. "You get your clothes on and come down to breakfast and I'll tell you all about it."

Gerry had not come upstairs to wake him, so he knew the dog had not come home. He swung his feet out of bed. He wiggled his toes, flopped his ankles around and was a little surprised that everything seemed to work and that he had suffered no damage from yesterday.

He washed hurriedly, and put on his school suit and his second-best shoes. School! It was Monday morning. Would there be any school? Well, certainly he was not going, not with the fire probably still raging and the streets engulfed in smoke. He hurried downstairs. As he slid into his chair at the breakfast table, he noticed that his mother had changed into another dress, and her hair was freshly combed, even though her face was pale and tired. Betty Ann had red-rimmed eyes, but she was trying to look cheerful.

"Nothing like a good breakfast to keep you going," Cora said, as she came in from the kitchen in a crisp gray uniform. She produced oatmeal with rich cream, and flannel cakes with molasses and fried ham. Cora thought that all the ills of the world could be cured by good food.

"Now, Mother," Betty Ann said, with a return of some of her usual good humor. "You've been out all night," she teased. "I think you should explain to your family."

Her mother laughed with the two children, and Cora hung around near the door, so she would not miss anything.

"It's all so simple," Mrs. Morton said. "I went to Aunt Matilda's. Uncle Will had gone down to his law office, to save his books and records, and she was alone."

She had stayed and helped her sister to pack her valuable possessions, for they thought the fire would reach Biddle Street. By the time they had been certain that there was no danger, at least for the moment, it was around four o'clock in the morning.

"Well," Mrs. Morton laughed. "I thought it would not be very ladylike to come strolling home at four o'clock in the morning. So Matilda and I just curled up in chairs and slept until it was daylight. Then, I didn't even wait for breakfast. I just had a cup of coffee and came home."

"Now, Mother," said Betty Ann, "if you had to stay out all night, I think you should have a more interesting story to tell. Wait until you hear what happened to Tod, and he was out only *half* the night." But Betty Ann didn't know the whole story, nor how long it would take to tell it. "Two nice old people brought him home in a wagon."

"Aw—ww, Betty Ann, I think we should get downtown," Tod said, but he was aching to tell all about his trip to the Harford Road.

"Yes, Tod, you're right. So let's start." But she remained seated at the table.

"That will be fine," his mother said, and her face brightened up. "Maybe you can be of some help to your father now. I'll give you some clean socks for him. You know how particular he is about his socks. Cora and I will make some sandwiches for you to take along."

"After we see that Dad is all right, I'll have to find the Western Union and report," Tod said. "I wonder where the Western Union is. I saw the Equitable Building blow up last night." Since Betty

Ann already knew the building was gone it wouldn't hurt her to hear what he had seen. "Of course, they must have had warning and gotten the operators out in time," he added. He hoped that what he was saying was true.

Then he told them about his panic and the people all running and the tolling of the bell, and about his long walk to Harford Road. Everybody laughed at his meeting with Ham, and about the head of the ghost that bounced off the tombstone.

Suddenly Tod heard a familiar little thump at the front door. It sounded just like the Sunpaper being delivered by his friend Charlie Matteson, but that couldn't be possible! Hadn't he seen the Sun Building in ruins last night?

Nevertheless, he raced to the front door, and there was Charlie going down the steps, and yes, there was the Sunpaper just outside their door.

"I brought your paper, Tod," he said, "because you're my friend. I couldn't get enough for the whole route. They were printed in Washington."

"Oh, thank you, Charlie," Tod said.

"They're getting twenty-five cents apiece for these papers at some places downtown. The *American* didn't publish at all today and the last I heard was that the *Herald* was still on its way here from Washington." Charlie hopped off the bottom step and hurried away.

Tod brought the paper into the dining room and gave it to his mother.

"Mike always calls it the Baltimore Sandpaper." Betty Ann caught her breath. "I wonder if he is all right."

Everyone clustered around Mrs. Morton as she read the news aloud. Tod pointed to a headline that said that dynamite had failed. It did not bring down the buildings, and often the fire leapfrogged, and ignited a spot a whole block away, so that the firemen could not tell what the results would be when they dynamited.

"Twenty-Four Blocks Burned in the Heart of Baltimore, City's most Valuable Buildings in Ruins," Mrs. Morton read and then she lowered the paper and looked at her children, "and it seems it is still out of control."

"Better get downtown fast," Tod said. "Betty Ann, you shouldn't have left Dad all alone."

"He wasn't alone. I told you that Sales came back," she said softly. "Poor Sales! When he came back he was carrying a bottle of cough medicine, home-made. His mother had made him bring it along and it was so big that it wouldn't fit in his pocket." Betty Ann laughed. "Anyhow his cough was better, and Dad insisted that I bring home some of the things that were in the safe. Dad said that I was so pretty that no one would think I was a very important person, carrying all that cash on me. Yes, I brought all the cash, and some of the most important papers. And no one bothered me. They say it is amazing that there is so little theft or looting in the city."

Betty Ann continued, with animation. "Can you imagine Sales coming back to help Dad? He begged Dad to leave the factory, but when Dad refused to go Sales stayed with him. We had a lot of time to talk and I got to know him much better."

"What about his mother? Didn't he feel she needed him?" Mrs. Morton asked. They all knew of Sales' devotion to his mother.

"Oh, he took care of his mother first. Sales told me about it."

"Betty Ann," Tod broke in, "hadn't we better get started?"

"Of course, Tod, of course," she said. "Just give me time to tell mother about this." Betty Ann went on with her story.

"Sales passed St. Leo's church and saw the Italian people frantic with fear. They were out in the street with all their possessions, getting ready to flee the city if the fire jumped Jones' Falls. With their hurdy-gurdies, too, imagine, and even the monkeys!"

Tod knew that usually a trained monkey accompanied the grind organ to attract the people, and to collect in their little hats all the pennies they could beg from the passersby.

Betty Ann went on talking.

"When Sales got to his home, he found his mother loading up Mrs. Saffield's landau with her belongings. You remember that Mrs. Donnella works for her as a housekeeper. The coachman said, 'Hurry up, Sales. You are to come along. We'll all go out to the Saffields' place in the Green Spring Valley. But for goodness' sake tell your mother to hurry.'

"Sales' mother was so excited that she couldn't find anything. She spent twenty minutes hunting for her best apron and never did find it. Sales finally got her things together for her and packed a few of his own belongings, for her to take to Mrs. Saffield's. But Sales himself had no intention of going to the Green Spring Valley."

Betty Ann then told how Sales explained to his mother that he must help Mr. Morton, but promised that he would take his cough medicine. Then he kissed his mother goodbye, content that she would be safe in the Green Spring Valley with Mrs. Saffield, and he would be free to go back to the factory.

Tod wished Betty Ann would hurry with the rest of her story. He was terribly interested in what she was telling them, but he was anxious to start downtown.

Sales had told her that the Italian people, who had thought they were safe in this new country, were now faced with the fear that they would lose their homes and all they possessed.

So they were prepared to flee the moment the fire jumped Jones' Falls. The pushcarts and the hurdy-gurdies were lined up in the streets near the church, with possessions wrapped in blankets or shawls inside the carts or sometimes hanging on the sides. Some threw clothes and bedding from their upstairs windows.

Men and women yelled at each other. Old people cried and scolded. The children, who had been fitted into the corners of the mattresses and bedding on the carts, screamed in fright, while the monkeys skittered from cart to cart.

They were ready to go—not quite sure where, but *somewhere* into the open country. But first they would pray, and they knelt in the littered streets.

The parish priest stood at the top of the church steps, and blessed them, blessed them all—people, carts, hurdy-gurdies, and the skittering monkeys. "Put your faith in God," he told them, "for he will protect you."

Again Tod interrupted Betty Ann's story.

"But Sales came back to the factory?"

"Yes, clasping his bottle of cough medicine in his hand," Betty Ann smiled. "But his cough seemed better. So then Dad sent me home with the most important things, including money. All right, let's get down to the factory, Tod. I'll get my coat and hat." She was wearing the same outfit she had worn yesterday, but Tod noticed that her brown dress had two big holes, scorched and ragged near the hem of her skirt.

As Betty Ann left the dining room, Tod looked out the window and saw Debbie Waid in the yard, coming up the walk. He rushed to the kitchen door and was there to let her in before she could give her timid knock, so lady-like that sometimes they could not hear it at all.

"Oh, Tod! You're all right!" she said, as if this was a surprise to her.

"Of course, I'm all right," he said. "Why wouldn't I be?"

"Well," said Debbie, "we heard all sorts of stories about your delivering Western Union messages all over the city—"

"Aw—w, I did deliver one—but—"

As usual Debbie looked newly scrubbed. Her bangs, exactly even across her forehead, in Buster Brown style, peeked out from under her white, knitted Tam-O-Shanter, that matched her spotless mittens.

"Tod had a pretty hard time of it, Debbie," said Cora, coming in from the dining room. She picked up the coal scuttle, and poured coal on the fire. "He went all the way out to Harford Road, walked, too, and had a terrible time getting home. A nice old couple brought him home in their wagon."

"Aw-w." He wished Cora would not talk so much.

"It's dreadful, Tod, isn't it?" Debbie said, her eyes big with alarm. "My father says the soldiers have been called out and that Governor Warfield came up from Annapolis last night—and—and—the Governor just asked for another train, and he got it right away, a train for himself and his staff—"

"Who said so?" Tod asked. "Where did you get all that stuff?"

"Oh, my Dad got it. You know doctors have a

way of finding out things." There was a glint of mischief in her eyes. "I know what you mean, though. You're so fusty! You mean if it came by telephone someone may have misunderstood what was said." She looked at him, and her amused little smile made her wrinkle her nose like a bunny rabbit. "You know that's just what I told my Dad—that you always say the telephone will never replace the telegraph."

He felt better now, because she agreed with him.

"But Dad says that at the hospital they are getting reports regularly by both telephone and telegraph."

Tod had never heard her talk so much.

"Dad didn't come home until early in the morning. All the doctors worked all night. There haven't been any people killed but they had to vac—vac—vac—"

"Evacuate?" Mrs. Morton, coming into the kitchen, supplied the word. Tod thought he had never seen his mother so tense and yet so calm. She must be anxious that he and Betty Ann get down to help their father, but she had not shown a bit of impatience.

"Yes, that's it, Mrs. Morton—e-vac-u-ate. Thank you. I know what it means. It means they are moving all the people from the City Hospital* for fear the fire may spread."

It was very quiet in the kitchen. Then a red hot

---

* Now Mercy Hospital.

coal spit and fizzled, and popped from the open grate to the floor. Cora grabbed the shovel and tucked the coal back in the fire. It was she who broke the silence.

"That sky, last night!" she said. "Like fiery dragons!"

"Or bombs bursting in the air," Mrs. Morton said softly.

"Oh-h!" Debbie said. "Do you think the sky looked like that when Francis Scott Key wrote *The Star-Spangled Banner?*"

"At least around Fort McHenry, I suppose," Mrs. Morton said, "and Fort McHenry survived, and so did Baltimore. And we've had other fires, too, and riots, and Baltimore was once called Mobtown, but we got over it! So I guess we will get over this!"

His mother could talk like this! Her head was held high. He suddenly found he was standing a little straighter, and he stuck his head up in the air!

"Mr. Morton is all right, isn't he?" Debbie asked. "We heard that the store burned down."

"We think he is all right, Debbie," Mrs. Morton said, and then in a whisper, "We hope so."

"Betty Ann and I are going right down to the factory," Tod said.

"To the factory! Oh, Tod! My father says that the fire will probably reach the Falls and your factory is right in its path. Oh, Tod! You'll be careful!" Her gaze went around the kitchen and Tod knew she was looking for Gerry.

"I'm sorry I couldn't help hunt for Gerry yesterday, Mrs. Morton," she said. "Dad took mother and me down to see the fire. He drove us down in the carriage, but we didn't stay long, because Dad had to get back to the hospital. It was late when we got home—too late to try to find Gerry. I'm sorry!"

"You can look today," Tod grinned. "Didn't Betty Ann tell you—oh, no you didn't see Betty Ann last night. Well, Gerry was locked up all that time in the store—in that little back room he always liked. No one knew he was there, until yesterday morning when Sales got into the store. Sales opened the door of that little room and Gerry shot out."

"Oh, but where is he? Didn't he come home?" Debbie said, but she already knew the answer. "Where on earth can he be? *Tod*, you don't think that Ham took him and locked him up for the night, just to scare you?"

"No, Debbie, no," Tod said quickly. Then when he saw her astonishment at his quick defense of Ham, he told her about their meeting last night at the Greenmount Cemetery.

"So you see, it would be almost impossible for Ham to do anything to Gerry," he finished.

"Well, it's all Ham's fault anyhow. He shouldn't have thrown poor Gerry with that lasso." Debbie said. "He scared Gerry and that was why he ran away."

"Well, Ham seemed real worried that Gerry was lost." Tod felt strange taking Ham's side in anything, and he hastened to justify it. "Ham said he would help us hunt for Gerry and he sounded like he meant it."

"You have so much to do, Tod. Shall I try to find Gerry for you?"

"Oh, would you, Debbie?" Tod said eagerly, "Maybe if you went around the neighborhood and called him and asked if anyone had seen him—?"

"Sure, Tod, I'll do that. Of course I will."

"And Debbie. I'm so afraid the police may get him. I don't think his license has been renewed. Dad promised to get it, but I'm not sure he did, and I just couldn't bother him yesterday with all he had on his mind. So Debbie—if the police—" he didn't know what to tell her. If the police had the dog, he didn't know what could be done.

"Poor Gerry!" Debbie sighed. "I'll bet he's trying to get home. He loves you, Tod, that dog does. Somebody must have tied him up or he'd be home." She put her hand on the doorknob. "I have some ideas about where he might be." She started out the back door, and looked back at him with a smile as bright as a summer day. Then she wrinkled her nose like a bunny rabbit.

"Girls are smarter than boys," she said. "I'll find Gerry for you."

Somehow, he thought that maybe she would.

12

Tod and Betty Ann had delayed so long that it was late in the morning when they finally left the house.

As soon as they were outside the front door they found themselves walking in a bluish haze. Overhead the sky was dark and threatening with belching clouds of black smoke. Tod had an awful feeling that the city was doomed. He coughed and wiped his eyes, and Betty Ann held her muff in front of her face.

Betty Ann carried the package that held socks for her father, and a supply of sandwiches. She refused to entrust it to Tod. They walked down Carrollton Avenue looking longingly for a cab, even though they knew there was little or no chance of finding one. No streetcars were running, so there was nothing to do but walk.

Going down Fayette Street they saw knots of people and heard bits of conversation. It was always along the same lines: ". . . best to get into the country," ". . . whole city will go." As they came closer to the fire, the people they saw looked bewildered. "So I came to work at the factory this morning, and there wasn't any factory," one man said. Some people seemed so dazed that they just stood looking at each other, or staring into space. Some wandered aimlessly about. "What should we do?" he heard one man say, and another said in a puzzled voice, "Where should we go?"

It was not until they had come to Howard Street that they had a view of the area, so badly devastated that the buildings had simply vanished. South as far as Lombard Street—east pushing out toward Jones' Falls, every structure had appeared. A spike here and there, a corner of a building—heaps and mounds of rubble, that was all there was left.

"The Continental went down in ten minutes," one of the soldiers on guard told them when they stopped to ask the best way to get to the factory. "It was the winds that did it. In these narrow streets, it blew a gale of fire that carried the flames."

Tod remembered that last night the winds had blown him through the streets with the suddenness and violence of a squall—a storm of fire.

"The wind changed all around," the soldier said. "First it was south and west. Then it grew stronger and at seven-thirty last night it had changed to west. Then at eleven o'clock it changed around to northwest."

"The Morton Factory, lady?" the soldier said in answer to Betty Ann's question. "Look, if it is already burning, or if it is about to go, you can't get anywhere near it." The soldier looked closely at Betty Ann's sad face and went on in a gentler tone. "Tell you what—" and he directed them to go around almost the same way they had gone yesterday, no doubt thinking they would be too discouraged by the distance to walk that far.

"Do you know where the Western Union is, sir?" Tod asked.

"Western Union?" the soldier rubbed his chin that bristled with yesterday's whiskers. "Western Union? You know you're the first one that has asked me that question this morning."

"Do you know where it is?" Tod persisted.

"No, son. No. Sorry."

They went up Howard Street, and Tod saw the familiar outlines of the old Lexington Market, untouched, looking just the same, except that only a few of the stalls had opened up. They continued north and crossed to Charles Street. They walked down Charles Street as they had done yesterday. They came to Clay Street, but what a different scene! It was completely empty of wagons, horses or drivers, and only a stray person or so moved in this spot of yesterday's stampede. The fire had not come this far north, nor had dynamite been used.

"Look, Betty Ann," Tod said. "The City Hall is safe, and the Post Office—and so are those other buildings."

"Thank goodness!" Betty Ann heaved a great sigh. "It all looked awfully bad last night."

"Sure did!" The voice of a fireman standing near

surprised them. His sooty face looked seamed with black creases of fatigue. "You see, the wind changed. That helped to save all of these buildings. Last night, not just the City Hall, but the Court House, the Post Office, and a lot of these buildings had bucket brigades on the roofs to put out any sparks or flying embers that fell on them. Even the *old* City Hall,* and the Zion Church next to it, were saved that way."

Tod and Betty Ann thanked the weary fireman, and cut over toward the east to reach the factory on Gay Street, and then turned south. It was not until they came to the barricades that marked off the danger zone that a soldier stopped them.

"You must have a pass to come through here," he informed them.

"Where do I get a pass?" Betty Ann asked.

"At the Court House," the soldier said.

"But," she said appealingly, "I've walked miles this morning. My father is in there trying to save his factory, The Morton Shoe."

"Oh, oh yes, The Morton Shoe." Tod thought he showed a little more interest. "But what help do you think you are going to be to him, Miss? This is a danger zone. Women aren't allowed in here, or children, either."

Hot blood flooded Tod's face! Children indeed!

---

* Built by Rembrandt Peale as the Peale Museum (the first museum in America) in 1814, and now restored to its original name and function.

He started to take out the paper with Mr. Dokings' signature on it, showing that he had real business with the Western Union, but he saw that Betty Ann was trying persuasion.

"My father has been in the factory all night long. Someone has got to go in and take these fresh socks to him, and this food. Please let me go through."

The soldier hesitated. He looked hard at Betty Ann and then he smiled and motioned her to come through.

"But you can't take the boy with you," he said.

"But Betty Ann, we have to find the Western Union," Tod pleaded.

"You go home and wait, Tod," she said as she looked back at him from inside the barricade.

"But Betty Ann." Tod felt he could not bear her desertion. "Don't you want to find Mike?"

"Oh, Tod! What can I do? I have to be sure that Dad is all right." Her eyes were filled with sudden tears, so maybe she really was sorry.

Yet she had certainly let him down, leaving him all alone and outside the lines. He was disgusted.

He stood for several minutes gazing longingly at the barrier, but never approaching the burly soldier who had refused him entrance.

He finally decided he would just have to find the Western Union office all by himself.

He reasoned that the Western Union must be working somewhere, and as close to the Equitable Building as possible, because all of the out-of-town wires were routed to the main office. Last night he had felt that everything was finished when the Equitable Building burned. But today he had had time to think of all the stories that Make had told him. The Western Union never slept! The Western Union carried on!

Somewhere the Western Union was doing business, if only he could find it. Wherever it was, it would have wires going into the office. Maybe that was the way to find the office!

He looked up and began to scan the wires overhead. Some of them looked like giant spider webs. There were stumps of half-burned telegraph poles, black and charred, sometimes with a few cross-bars that had escaped; but any wires he could see were twisted and broken.

Yet, surely the Western Union had not gone out of business. Somewhere there *must* be an office! Somewhere there *must* be wires.

He walked around the outside of the closed-off area. If he could see wires, wires that were still up, wires that led somewhere, he could follow them to the Western Union.

Finally he saw what he was looking for—wires that were strung from pole to pole, and did not sag too much. They went straight into the burned-out area, and they continued as far as he could see. These were wires that were working, of that he was sure. His knowledge gave him confidence as he approached a soldier at the corner.

"Please, sir," he said very politely, "I am trying to get to the Western Union. I delivered a message last night in this emergency, and I must report back to the Western Union."

"Burned out," the soldier said and turned away.

"But, sir, the Western Union is always open."

"Nobody knows where anything is, sport. Why don't you just go home?" The soldier looked tired and miserable.

"But please, sir," Tod knew he must be very polite and not get the soldier mad at him. "Please, sir, will you look at those wires?" Tod pointed overhead. "They must lead to the Western Union. They *must*. And you wouldn't want to keep me from reporting." He pulled the paper from his pocket. "Look! This is where the man signed his name."

"Harford Road!" The soldier looked at the paper and then at Tod. "You had to walk out there, didn't you?"

"Yes. I was out almost all night. So you see it is important that the Western Union knows that the message was delivered. I'm sure those wires lead to the office."

"You know you're a smart kid." He squinted at the wires overhead. "Go ahead!"

Tod darted inside the forbidden area. He followed the wires, but he had no idea as to where he was exactly because everything had been burned down. He went to one of the poles, standing tall and straight, and put his ear against it, and he knew he was right, for the wires were singing! Nobody seemed to know why they sang, but Tod felt very certain that singing wires meant messages were being sent, and that they would surely lead him to the office!

He followed the wires, looking up at them until he felt his neck was broken. He began to see buildings that were still standing, and then, still following the wires, he came outside of the barriers. Suddenly he saw a place where the old wires had been spliced into the new shiny wires! He was sure that the Western Union linemen had done a job on these wires, just lately—probably this morning—and he knew for certain that he had found the Western Union.

He came to the corner of Saratoga and Guilford Avenues and he recognized the House of Welsh, a well-known restaurant. The wires led straight into the building.

Even before he reached the entrance, he saw the familiar blue uniforms on the messenger boys going in and out of the House of Welsh. He followed one of the messengers into the building. Crowds of people were being served on the first floor.

He followed the messenger up the steps to the second floor and then to the third floor, and it was then that he heard the welcome tap, tap, tap of the telegraph.

He had found it. The fire, the loss of the store, the worry about his father, even Gerry's disappearance faded for a moment as he stood in the doorway and saw the operators at work.

The city might be burning up, but the Western Union worked on. The singing wires were sending out the story of the Baltimore Fire to the whole world. This little spot held the telegraphers who tapped out their stories, and risked their lives for the privilege.

The Western Union! Tod felt a thrill of pride! He had delivered a message, and returned to make his report. He was now a part of the Western Union Telegraph Company.

13

On this third floor of The House of Welsh, Tod saw the sending and receiving machines set up in every available spot, on tables and dressers and chests. The telegraphers sat on chairs or stools or even turned-over wooden boxes: some were standing with no place to sit. Two cot beds were pushed against the wall, and these held sleeping men and a few sitting on the ends of the cots.

At first Tod could not find Mike. Then he saw him in a corner of the room, his fingers furiously working a key, his black hair dissheveled and falling over one eye.

Mike looked up and a flash of surprise broke over his face as he saw Tod and beckoned to him. "Wait until I finish this message," he said, as Tod hurried over to him. In a few minutes Mike pushed back his chair and went over to one of the cots and poked the sleeping man. "Take my wire for me, will you?" Mike said.

"Sure, sure," the man grumbled and jumped as if a pin had been stuck in him. "But you don't need to scare a man to death," he grinned, and fell groggily into Mike's chair.

There were so many things that Tod wanted to tell Mike. First, of course, about delivering the message on Harford Road. And he told him about Teddy, and about the "ghost," and showed him the man's signature. He felt it was worth everything he had gone through, when Mike clapped him on the shoulder and said, "So you're a real messenger boy now."

Quickly Tod told about the store burning up, only to find that Mike knew all about it. Then Tod told him that Betty Ann had sent her best regards, and Mike asked many questions about her.

At last Mike took him to the Superintendent of Messengers to report the delivery of his message. The Superintendent put a hand on Tod's shoulder and said, "We wondered what had happened to Teddy." He smiled mysteriously. "Do you know what was in that message?" Tod said nothing because he was afraid that Teddy should not have told him. "Of course, usually we are not allowed to say," the Superintendent went on, "but now that you are one of us, I can tell you that the message called out one of the men in the Dandy Fifth—that's the Fifth Regiment. So you see, Tod, you too helped in this fight against the fire."

And Tod was happier than he had ever been in his life.

They went over to a corner of the room, where

Mike found a stool for him, while he himself perched on a spindly chair that looked as if it might collapse at any minute. Tod told Mike about finding the Western Union by following the wires.

"I saw the Equitable Building last night with flames shooting out in every direction, and Mike, I—I—was worried." Tod wiped his hand over his eyes remembering those awful moments. "Mike, I was afraid something had happened to *you*." He touched Mike's hand as if to be sure that Mike was there beside him.

"I'm tough!" But Mike's eyes were warm and gentle behind his gold-rimmed glasses. "Why? I'm a telegrapher!" and his wide grin showed his delight in his job.

Some of the telegraphers had gathered around, and they all talked as if Tod was one of them now, and therefore should know everything that had happened.

"After we fled from the Equitable Building," Mike said, "we hunted down the wires and found we could get the lineman to rig up an outside wire to the branch office at Gay and Lombard Streets."

"All the newspaper men were trailing around with us," one of the operators put in. "You see, the newspaper men had one of the biggest stories that had ever come out of Baltimore, and they couldn't get it on the wire, so they followed us."

"So we finally got a wire out of the branch office

at Gay and Lombard," Mike took up the story, "and we were doing fine—just fine—getting the story out."

The other operators began to laugh.

"Then it got hot," one of them said as they all laughed, "but it had been cold when we went into the office, so we had all kept our overcoats on."

"The manager knew that the fire was coming closer," Mike continued, "and he wanted us to give up and get away. He kept on saying, 'Get out! You'll burn up!' but we paid no attention. We were sending out the biggest story we had ever had. The newspaper men were right beside us yelling their stories at us, so we could put them on the wire."

The men all laughed, living those moments over again.

"It got hotter and hotter as the fire came closer, but we kept right on sending. The manager yelled, 'Tell 'em N.M. Tell 'em N.M.'" Tod knew that N.M. meant "No More."

"We heard funny noises—crackling, sizzling, the building was on fire—the top part of it. So we grabbed everything we could—hats, coats, telegraph machines, typewriters, anything we could get our hands on, and anything we could carry. And we got out just in time. In a matter of minutes the building went up with a whoosh!" Mike finished with a laugh and the rest of the telegraphers laughed uproariously, as if almost being burned to death was a very funny joke.

Then they had nowhere to go. After some fumbling around, the linemen found they could get lines into the House of Welsh, and Martin J. Welsh, Senior, told them they could use his restaurant as long as they needed it.

Mike thought there were about thirty-five operators, doing the best they could in this little third-story room, telling the world the story of the fire.

Quick and pounding footsteps came up the stairs, and a messenger boy dashed into the room, yelling as he came, "Say, what do you think?" The boy was breathless and he began to cough.

A gray-haired operator slapped the boy on the back and said, "Now try to get your breath, first. You ought to know there's too much going on in the Western Union ever to get excited about *anything*. Wear yourself out, you will. Now count ten and then tell us what's wrong. Are we about to be dynamited, burned up, or just moved to another location?"

The boy coughed, gulped, and then told his news, with the words falling over each other. Thomas O'Neill, a red-headed Irishman whose department store at Charles and Lexington Streets was one of the best in the city, had defied the firemen, and the policemen, when they wanted to dynamite his store to head off the fire. He had taken his stand in the center aisle of his drygoods store, and said they would have to blow him up with the store.

The very special news was that the fire had not

touched the O'Neill store but had leapfrogged over it.

The old operator looked at the boy. "Is that the best you can do? Boy, you just came on duty, didn't you?"

"Yes, sir," the boy looked embarrassed.

"Well, you're forgiven, then. But that so-called news about Tom O'Neill is at least twelve hours old, *at least*. Don't ever come into the Western Union with reports as old as *that*, and call it news."

"That's not all the story!" the boy insisted. "Do you know *why* O'Neills didn't burn down?"

"Sure," the operator said, "O'Neill's didn't burn because Tom O'Neill had a special sprinkling system in his store and it worked."

"There's something else," the messenger boy said. "You didn't know that Tom O'Neill took a carriage up to the Carmelite Convent at Biddle Street to ask the nuns to pray that his business would be saved. You see," the boy said triumphantly, "that's news! You didn't know that!"

Now it was the turn of the gray-haired operator to be taken aback, as the other telegraphers broke into good-natured laughter.

Another messenger came into the room and came straight to Mike.

"Your mother sent you some clothes, your lunch, with plenty of extra sandwiches, and a whole cake," he said as he handed Mike a hat-box that looked heavily laden. "She said she was sure the operators were starving to death. And Mr. Treadwell, your mother says he's not there. The dog, you know. Your mother says he's gone."

"What happened?" Mike jumped up from the chair. "Did mother say she left the gate open? How could the dog get out?"

Tod was listening to every word.

"Your mother says she was away from the kitchen just for a few minutes," the boy said. "And when she came back, the dog wasn't there. She went out to the gate, and she called and called but the dog was gone. Just disappeared."

"Was the gate left open?"

"No, she says it wasn't. But it wasn't latched, either. She had to leave it unhooked for the garbage man, but anybody could open it."

"Tod," Mike turned away from the messenger, "of course it's Gerry we're talking about."

"But Mike," Tod said, puzzled and angry. "I've been scared to death that Gerry was hurt or dead. Why didn't you let us know?"

"I meant to, I really did." Mike looked very unhappy. "Of course I had no idea that the whole city was going up in smoke."

"But Mike, we had already lost Gerry once. Then Sales found him locked in that little back room. Poor Gerry!" And once started, Tod told Mike how the delivery boy had saved the valuables in the safe by using the combination that he wasn't supposed to know, and how Gerry had come bounding out of the door of the back room when Sales opened the door.

"Good old Sales!" Mike said. "Quite a boy, that Sales! Now about Gerry, I ran into him right near our house, after I had been called out to work because of the fire. I couldn't understand what he was doing running around loose with a big fire raging, so I took him home." Mike heaved a big sigh, and acted as if he had come to a great decision.

"Well—let's face it, Tod, I had an idea, a really good idea, but I didn't know that the fire was going to go on all day and all night, and that Gerry would be among the missing." He hesitated as if he hated to go on, and his words came as if they were being wrenched out of him. "You see, Betty Ann and I had a fight."

"That's what Betty Ann said." Yet Tod could still not quite understand it. So they had a fight—but why should that turn good old dependable Gerry into a disappearing dog?

"But, Mike—what has that got to do with locking Gerry in your yard?"

"I know, kid," Mike groaned. "I deserve anything you say to me. Anything! Women! You steer clear of them, my boy. Women!"

"I think you and Betty Ann are both crazy!" Tod said. "Now you've lost Gerry! Where do you think he is?"

"I don't know. Honest, sport, I don't know."

155

Tod had never seen Mike so sad and woebegone, and he remembered that Mike probably hadn't had any sleep for two days. He was sorry for him. But why—*why* hadn't Mike let them know about the dog last night? Last night? No, maybe it had been impossible. Too many things had been happening last night.

"You know what we fought about?" Mike said, so humbly that Tod could hardly believe it was Mike speaking. "I guess it's important to girls. She got mad because I couldn't take her to Sally's house last night. Not only that but I couldn't even promise her when I would have a day off or a night, even. But a man's got to do his duty. *You* know how this business is. *You* know that telegraphers can never count on being off on any Saturday or Sunday or holiday. You know that, Tod, but Betty Ann—well," and Mike put his hand to his head.

"Then when I spotted Gerry, I got this idea! Anyhow, *I* thought it was brilliant! I collared Gerry and put him in our yard. I planned I would work Sunday, but I'd be off at night and not too late to see your sister. So I'd take Gerry back to your house, surprise Betty Ann, and I could take her to Sally's a little bit late. Betty Ann would be so happy to see Gerry that it would be easy to make up.

"So what happens?" Mike's voice was angry now. "The whole blooming city burns up!"

"And Sally never had her party, because of the fire," Tod said.

"She didn't? Well, then maybe Betty Ann is not so mad at me—"

"Maybe you should find out," Tod said, not wanting to break Betty Ann's confidence, but wanting to console Mike. "She said if I saw you, I was to give you her very best regards."

"She *did*?" Tod thought that Mike looked like a drowning man who had just been thrown a life preserver.

Tod talked about Betty Ann bringing home the valuables that had been in the safe, and how they feared that the factory might be in danger.

Before Mike had a chance to reply, a messenger rushed into the office and came straight to Mike.

"You said to let you know if we heard anything about that block of buildings where the Morton Factory is—"

"Yes-ss." Mike looked at Tod.

"The fire has already reached there. That row of buildings will go any minute."

"Come on, Tod. You say Betty Ann is down there with your father?"

Mike went to get his overcoat. "Schmitty!" he called to a man Tod knew was one of the managers. "Going out. Personal business. The Morton Factory may go any minute." He was halfway to the door, with Tod sprinting after him.

Mike led the way down the stairs. His long strides took him straight toward the fire, with Tod trying to keep up with him. He passed the barricade and kept his pass out for the soldiers to see as he raced along. Nobody questioned Tod because Mike always said "Western Union," and included Tod with a wave of his hand.

"You see, Tod"—Mike spoke disjointedly as they hurried along—"There are some things that we just have to accept. Evidently there is nothing to do about the factory if the fire has reached it. Of course, they'll get Betty Ann and your father out in time. Of course they will!" Mike put his hand to his face. He coughed and his voice was hoarse. "Well, good Lord above us. I hope they get them out in time. Anyhow we'll be there shortly."

Tod did not answer. They were climbing over a heap of rubble, and it was all he could do to keep up with Mike.

14

Tod was coughing from the smoke, and Mike was gasping for breath as they climbed over fallen brick and mortar, and skirted twisted skeletons of steel and concrete that had once been buildings. They walked through a wasteland, where Tod could see nothing at all that he recognized in this neighborhood that he had known so well.

Soldiers, seeing Mike's pass, waved on both Mike and Tod. Only once did a soldier stop them. He grabbed Mike's arm, and slapped at his trousers down near the shoe tops, and Mike discovered it was not only the ruins that were smoking but also the cuffs of his very best pants.

As they neared the factory, it seemed to Tod that everything to the west had been destroyed. The block where the factory loomed seemed to be intact, but the smoke swirling over roof tops showed that the fire had already touched these buildings. Few people were on the street. Here and there a man scurried along as if in a desperate hurry.

No fire engines were to be seen as they came to the door of the factory. No hose criss-crossed the

159

cobblestones. The firemen were there, but they were busy rolling up the hose. Evidently all hope of saving this block had been abandoned.

The factory itself looked different. The big sign saying "The Morton Shoe" dropped crookedly to one side and seemed about to fall. Smoke and soot had smudged the cheerful red brick building to the ugly darkness of an old derelict.

The door was open and water gushed over the threshold. They waded in and Tod felt the chill of the water coming through his shoe laces, and over the tops of his shoes.

"Betty Ann! Betty Ann!" Mike shouted.

Unlit and gloomy, the stockroom looked at first as if it were crowded with soldiers and firemen only. It was a moment before Tod could see that they were all there—his father, Betty Ann and Sales. He had an instant of pure joy in seeing they were safe, before he realized how hopeless their situation was. His father stood ankle-deep in water. There were spots of soot on his face and his eyes were red. He still wore his derby with the crown burned out. His tie was neatly tied, even though the shirt under it had a big hole in it.

Betty Ann stood beside him, straight and determined. Her little brown muff was pushed together, rumpling the fur and showing how tightly her hands must be clenched together, inside her muff. Under one arm she still held the paper bag she had brought from home, but it looked almost empty.

Sales was shivering and his lips were blue with cold even though his overcoat had the collar turned up around his neck. He held tight to a cardboard shoebox, as he juggled one of Mrs. Morton's sandwiches, trying to eat it without dropping it.

Tod and Mike sloshed inside. Mike went directly to Betty Ann, and Tod to his father's side. Sales nodded to him as he tried for another bite of sandwich, and his father put a hand on his shoulder. There was no chance for talk. Soldiers and firemen had taken over and had evidently been trying to get all of them to leave.

"You've got about five minutes, Mr. Morton," a soldier said. "Be sure you take the most important things—records—that sort of stuff."

"Sales has all the remaining papers of any importance in the shoebox," Mr. Morton said.

"All these shoes," the janitor said, as he looked at the shelves loaded with spring stock. "They must be worth a lot of money."

"Yes, a lot of money," Mr. Morton said quietly.

"Can't you take some of them along?"

"No."

"Why not?" the janitor said.

"Because of my insurance policy. I think there is a clause in it about not removing any of the stock from the premises if I want to collect the insurance."

"That's crazy!" exclaimed the janitor. "All those good shoes! Half of Baltimore will be barefooted tomorrow. You'd make a fortune. I could use a pair myself." He reached out and took down two boxes.

"Put them down!" said Mr. Morton.

"Hanged if I will." The man raised his voice so that the other men could hear him. "Why don't you all take some? In another five minutes all these shoes will be gone—burned up! Come on! Don't be chumps! Each one of you take a few pairs."

No one moved.

"You're the chump!" a soldier finally said. "Do you want to get shot for looting?" His hand went to his gun.

"It won't be looting if the owner gives them to us." He looked at Mr. Morton slyly. "We could all come and pay you later," he grinned.

"Dad, why should you waste them?" Tod said. "All these shoes! Letting them all burn up—"

His father's tired eyes turned to him.

"Remember you are the owner's son, Tod."

"Take them! Take them!" Suddenly Tod felt wild. He rushed to the shelves and began loading his arms with boxes. "These are your shoes, Dad, let's save some of them."

"You are sure, Tod?" his father's voice was discouraged.

Tod faced his father, standing there in his battered derby, water up over his ankles, his face soot-covered, and he wondered how his father could possibly look so dignified—more than that—he looked almost noble.

"But—but Dad—" his voice was a little uncertain

now. "Why should we leave them here to be burned up?"

"Because of a little piece of paper called an insurance policy—a contract—" his father said.

Contract? Tod stood with three pairs of beautiful shoes under his arm—his own size. He looked longingly at the shelves crammed with boxes and boxes of shoes—thousands of shoes that no one would ever wear. Not only the shoes. He cast one glance at the old rolltop desk that he would never see again. He gave a quick look at the deserted baby carriage for the last time.

Sadly, he dropped the boxes of shoes into the eddying water. He turned toward the door.

"We will take nothing," his father said firmly, and he stood a little straighter, a little taller as he looked at Tod.

"Come on, Mr. Morton," Sales said.

"You lead the way, sweetheart," Mike said to Betty Ann, as he caught her to him in a quick hug, and it seemed right and proper for Mike to call his sister by the endearing name.

Tod and Sales walked on either side of Mr. Morton, each linking an arm in one of his, with Betty Ann and Mike leading the way.

The water made little swishing sounds as they waded to the door. Once outside, a gust of smoke and soot blew in their faces. They coughed and choked, but they did not stop. They went as fast as the littered streets would allow. Mr. Morton was breathing heavily, but aside from that he walked with strength and purpose, and kept steady pace with the rest of them.

Tod's eyes were filled with smoke and tears, and he was sure he would never get rid of this smell of smoke. His wet feet made him shiver in the icy wind. Yet he broke out in perspiration whenever his head and face were enveloped in a heat blast, hotter than any midsummer day. He had his one glove on—he could not find the other one. His cap, his best one, he pulled down as far as he could, and wished for his old stocking cap. He took out his handkerchief to wipe his eyes. It was filthy with soot, yet he used it for want of something better.

They plodded on. Everything was gone—the store—the factory—the fireproof Equitable Building. The flames seemed determined to devour the entire city. They felt their way over uneven ground, over streets cluttered with every sort of rubbish. They went around heaps of smoldering ruins. They walked through cinders still hot, and always there was the fire at their heels.

"Will it never end?" Betty Ann said in despair. "Is the whole city going?"

"The whole city," Sales muttered in his croaking voice. "There won't be any more Baltimore."

"They have some plan to try to stop it at Jones' Falls," Mike said. Tod thought how educated Mike was because he didn't say it the way most Baltimoreans did, "Joneses Falls." Then Tod felt very guilty

164

that he could think of such little things at a time like this.

"We'll head for Welsh's," Mike said. "We can get something to eat there, and I can go back to work. And Betty Ann, we'll surely find someone who can drive your father home, and you, too."

"Thank you, Mike," Betty Ann said. "I guess the boys will have to walk home. Sales, you'll come and stay with us, of course. We'll find a way to let your mother know where you are."

Sales said something that sounded like "thank you," but a fit of coughing seized him. As his breath came back to him, he shifted the shoebox to his other arm and said something, but he was so hoarse that they could hardly hear him.

"I can't, Miss Morton," they finally heard Sales say. "Thank you just the same but I'll have to go back to our house. My mother was so excited that she forgot her landing papers, the deed to my father's grave—"

They all stopped and stared at Sales as if he had lost his mind. Hadn't his mother taken all her valuables to Mrs. Saffield's? What was Sales talking about?

"Sales," Mr. Morton said gently, "the Italian section of the city may be the next to go. You won't be allowed anywhere near your house."

"No doubt the soldiers are already keeping people away," Mike said.

"But Sales," Betty Ann said, "you told us that

your mother had taken her things to Mrs. Saffield's." Betty Ann linked her arm in his. "Come on, Sales, you come along home with us."

"What makes you think your mother left anything valuable at your house?" Tod asked.

"My mother sent word through the firemen, maybe it was by telephone." Sales gave Tod a shy little grin, when he said the word "telephone." "We both forgot, because these things were hidden away in a special place. I know where they are."

They had stopped in order to talk to Sales. Now, undecided, they stood around him, reluctant to let him go back into the fire, yet just as unwilling to insist that he could not go.

"Sales," Mike said very decisively, "when did you eat last?"

"Oo—hh!" Sales looked surprised, and then shocked. "Miss Betty Ann, that sandwich you gave me—I dropped the last of it before I left the factory."

"So when did you eat last?" Mike persisted.

"You're right, Mike," Mr. Morton said. "He had some coffee this morning, and if he did not finish that sandwich, he hasn't had anything much to eat today."

"Oo—hh! Oo—hh!" Sales sounded as if he were in mortal pain and they all came closer to him, ready to catch him if he was sick, or hurt. "Oo—hh! My bottle! I left it at the factory."

"His cough syrup!" Betty Ann said softly.

"Sales!" Mike said, very low and very positive. "You've taken care of the Mortons and forgotten about yourself. Now it's your turn to be taken care of. Come on. We're going to Welsh's."

"But Mr. Treadwell." Sales' scratchy voice was getting worse without his cough medicine. "It's shorter if I leave from here."

"Sales," Mike said sternly, his dark eyes steady and determined behind his glasses. "Haven't you noticed that every once in a while a soldier pops up and I show him my pass and I say we are getting out as fast as possible? Now you come along with us and we'll get to Welsh's and get some food. Then I'll see if I can get you a pass. The Western Union can do some amazing things in emergencies. I'll get you that pass—that is, if it is not *too dangerous.*"

"Thank you, Mr. Treadwell," he gave Mike his quiet smile, "and—and a cup of coffee will sure taste good."

They walked on. For the moment they had thought of nothing except Sales' predicament. Now they turned their faces in the direction of Welsh's and they were conscious, once more, of mortar and bricks from toppled buildings, and of streets that looked no different from all the rest of the rubble and debris. They were in a world of smoke and cinders and ruins.

15

Mike led the way, guiding them as best he could toward the House of Welsh. Even he seemed doubtful at times of his direction, because the streets were no longer passageways, but heaps of rubble that they must either go around or else climb over, risking the smoking embers.

Betty Ann and Tod stayed near their father, and Sales came last, hugging close the pasteboard shoebox.

They went as fast as they could, but now they were obliged to stop at times, to be sure that Mr. Morton could go on. He hardly said a word, but his breathing was so heavy that they were all conscious of it. Once in a while he would gasp for breath. His feet dragged at times with fatigue and discouragement.

If only he could tell his father that his love for him was greater than ever! If only he could let his father know that he understood his great loss! All he could do was to take his father's arm and help him over the worst spots.

They came from behind the barricades, and Tod

knew they must be near the House of Welsh. They came closer, and Tod saw the sign.

They had reached the haven of the restaurant. A little cluster of men moved aside for them to enter. Mike pushed open the door and they stumbled into the warmth and comfort of the steamy room. The welcome smell of food came to Tod, and over and above it, the aroma of coffee. Every table on this first floor was crowded, and Tod saw a few men that he knew by sight.

Everyone in the room turned to see who had come in. At one table, all the men stood up, motioning Betty Ann and Mr. Morton to take the table. Their eyes were full of sympathy as one man helped Mr. Morton to a place, and another pulled out a chair for Betty Ann. Cups of coffee were thrust into their hands, as they all sat down. Warmed and refreshed, they began to eat the sandwiches that were set before them.

A man, red-eyed and disheveled, came in, grabbed his hat from his head, looked around and then made his way to the Mortons' table.

He stuck out his hand and said to Mike.

"I'm Harry Stetson—remember me? Postal Telegraph?"

Mike looked blank for a moment and then smiled as he recalled, "Sure. We met during the campaign to elect Edwin Warfield as governor. How is the Postal Telegraph making out?"

"Well, the Postal Telegraph got burned out, too. But we managed to set up emergency headquarters at Forest and Orleans Streets. Only trouble is we don't have a built-in restaurant like you folks here at the Western Union. You're lucky! Think I'll go over there where there's a place at that table. Be seeing you."

Mike turned back to their table, and in a few minutes left without explanation.

When he came back, he brought word that he had sent a telegram to Debbie's father, Dr. Waid, at the hospital, to ask if a carriage could be found to take Mr. Morton and Betty Ann home. He was sure that Dr. Waid could manage something.

"And Sales, the fire hasn't reached your section of the city yet," Mike said. "Everybody in your neighborhood is packed and ready to leave if it is necessary. Do you still want that pass?"

"Oh yes, Mr. Treadwell. I must get those papers," Sales said.

"All right, Sales. The fire may reach there before you do, but I'll get it for you."

"And for me, too, Mike." Tod had not even known he was going to speak. But how could he possibly let Sales go alone, after all that Sales had done for the Mortons?

"You, Tod?" Mike said, as he looked at Mr. Morton.

Tod fully expected that either his father or Betty

Ann would object, but neither of them said anything. Perhaps all the Mortons felt a bit to blame that Sales had hurried his mother too much, because he wanted to get back to the factory.

It was now the Mortons' turn to help Sales. Neither his father or Betty Ann could do it, so he was to be trusted to fulfill the obligations of the family.

"I'll explain to Mother, Tod," Betty Ann said, nice as pie, "and be sure to bring Sales home with you."

Mike disappeared again, and when he came back this time he had passes for both the boys.

"Now, listen, you two," Mike said. "You know you can go around the fire and not be in too much danger, don't you?"

Tod looked at Sales and they both smiled. They knew the whole section so well they felt they could get there blindfolded.

"How do you feel, Sales?" Mike asked.

"That coffee helped. Guess I can keep on going, now."

"All right. I have some news for you," he included all of them as he began to explain. "It may be that the dirty, miserable little stream called Jones' Falls is going to save the city. Anyhow, they will make a last-ditch stand there. All the firemen, all the equipment, thirty-seven fire engines, all that are still in working order, are being massed right now at Jones' Falls. The stream is only about seventy-five

172

feet wide. If it jumps the Falls, there won't be much left of the city."

"That must be right near my house—" Sales said.

"I guess so," Mike said, and looked at Sales for a moment. "Sales, your house may be gone by the time you get there. Or it may be that there will be soldiers all over the place and they won't let you through even with your pass."

"No matter what happens, Mr. Treadwell—well —thanks." Sales stood up. "Tod, are you sure you want to go?"

"Yes, absolutely sure," Tod said.

"I'll take the box, Sales," Betty Ann said. "It will be safe with me. I'll get a ride home with Dad."

Mr. Morton seemed to come out of his daze as he watched Betty Ann take the box. It was the first sign of interest he had shown since coming into the restaurant.

"Let me have the box," he said, pulling it over close to him. But what could possibly be in the box that would be of any importance at this time?

Sales started to untie the string around the box but his fingers were too stiff, and Mike cut the cord with his pen knife.

Mr. Morton lifted the lid, surveyed the contents, and began to leaf through the papers and envelopes that filled the box. A flicker of a smile came over his face as he pulled an envelope from the box and out of it dropped—a dog tag.

Smilingly Mr. Morton took the document and

the dog tag and passed them over to Tod. "You thought I'd forgotten, didn't you? Here's Gerry's license. I meant to bring it home."

So Gerry was "legal," after all.

"Poor Gerry!" Betty Ann said, "Now we have the license but we haven't any dog!"

Mike looked at Tod and put his finger to his lips, in a gesture that commanded him to say nothing. If Mike did not want Betty Ann to know that he, Mike, had locked Gerry in his yard and then lost him again, if that was the way that Mike wanted it—well—. But poor Gerry! Where was he?

"I'll help you find him," Sales said. "We'll both hunt. We'll find him. Don't you worry, Tod."

Tod blinked back his tears. You could cry when you were worried about your father—or about Mike. But you couldn't cry about a dog. Or could you? To hide his tears he rose from the table.

"Come on, Sales, let's go," he said.

"I've forgotten," his father murmured. "So many things have happened. Gerry is still lost, isn't he?"

Tod nodded his head, and thanked his father again for the dog tag, as he put it in his pocket.

"Now, don't lose your passes," Mike said as he hurried them along.

Once again they went into the smoke-filled streets. They walked north and then east. In this way they avoided the area that was burning, but soot and ashes showered down on them.

Yesterday there had been confusion and much activity as people tried to save what they could. Today, everyone they saw had a look of despair, and there seemed to be only devastation and hopelessness.

As soon as they reached the other side of the Falls all this changed. On the eastern side of Jones' Falls there seemed a spirit of effort, a trying to do *something—anything* to save a dying city.

Tod looked at the firemen, weary and dirty. He knew that they had been on duty all night and all the day before. They had had no sleep and little rest. They had lived on sandwiches and coffee, often provided by bystanders. Yet these firemen were now busy massing the fire equipment on the east side of the Falls, and on the bridges. With no apparent slowing down, these men were fighting the fire as hard as ever.

As Mike had said, a wall of firemen, hoses and fire engines was massed on the east side of the Falls, and on the bridges. Streams of water from all the hose were turned toward the buildings on the west shore. Sometimes there was a good, true stream of water, sometimes it was but a trickle. Tod saw one of the firemen being rowed across the Falls in a small boat with a hose under his arm. Other firemen waded in water—water that was touched with ice here and there. But by getting down into the icy water they could get the hose closer. Could it be that the Jones'

175

Falls that had always been the butt of the jokes in Baltimore—could it be that this dirty, muddy stream would be the barrier that stopped the fire?

"If they stop the fire here," Tod said, "we won't have to get those papers, will we?"

They were down as far as Lombard Street. The fire engines on the bridge here sucked up water from the bed of the stream. Tod could hear the crackle and roar of the fire and the steady pump, pump, pump of the fire engines.

A yell! The bridge was on fire. If they were forced off the bridge, the fire had won! The grim and dirty-faced firemen refused to retreat. Together they advanced on the flames. Doggedly they turned hose on the burning spot. They refused to be driven back. They refused to fail. They stood and battled!

The bridge held. The pump, pump, pump of the engines seemed very loud.

Tod didn't know when it was that he noticed there seemed to be no new buildings catching fire. And every bridge was holding.

The angry, black, billowing smoke died down a little, leaving soft gray clouds and white plumes of steam.

The boys walked on to where they could see one of the largest buildings that still burned like a great torch. This was the building of the American Ice Company, and its storage shed. Every floor was packed with ice. The fire burned so fiercely that it seemed as if the ice itself were burning. The roof was gone, and the heat had fused and packed the ice into one great iceberg.

Tod saw a fireman holding a hose and yelling like a wild man to the other firemen, "Come on, boys, she's almost under control. Just a little more water—" As he shouted, disaster overtook him. A flaming ember dipped from the sky and struck his coat. Flames shot up. The other firemen quickly came to his rescue, pummeling him good-naturedly. They tore off his coat and wrapped him in a blanket and led him away.

As they passed Tod and Sales, the two boys could see the fireman's face black and sooty like a man in a minstrel show. But he had a broad grin, showing white teeth, and this was the first smile that Tod had seen on a fireman's face the whole day long.

His comrades sat the fireman down on one of the doorsteps, and no one paid any attention to his loud insistence that the fire was under control, and that it would be out in no time. Still protesting that the fire was practically out, the fireman fell asleep even as he talked.

There were fewer flames, and less belching of black smoke, not so many flying embers, and *no new fires*. The flames had not jumped Jones' Falls.

"I guess we've really got her licked." A fireman standing near Tod said it softly, almost like a prayer. "Baltimore is saved, I think."

Tod caught his breath. His city, his great city of Baltimore, lay humbled in devastation, its heart in rubble and cinders.

Then he saw the American Ice Building catch a fleeting ray of sunlight. From the gleaming tower of packed ice, there flashed millions of dancing and dazzling sunbeams, like a beacon of hope over the ruined city.

16

"Do you really think it is over?" Tod said, as they walked toward Sales' house through streets peopled with firemen, soldiers and policemen.

"Over?" a dirty-faced fireman answered them, as he slammed a hose coil on coil. "It will smolder for days, for weeks maybe. But we saved the city. It's all under control now."

Tod was so tired he could hardly put one foot after the other. He knew that Sales must feel even worse, for he had had no sleep at all last night, and he coughed more and more.

"Maybe it will be safe for me to stay home now," Sales said. "First, I'll be sure those papers are where we left them, and then—" His face was unnaturally white under the spots of soot.

They reached St. Leo's Church. The street was filled with people, with pushcarts, and children, and hurdy-gurdies. There was a buzz of talk, but nothing loud and no excitement. Everyone seemed to be waiting.

"Do you think they know that the fire has been stopped?" Tod said.

"Guess not. The news hasn't reached them yet," Sales said, as they came to his doorstep.

Sales took out his key and they entered the little house. Tod had never been here before and he thought how pretty everything looked. He was surprised to see that the rooms were so small that it made the furniture look much too big.

Sales ran upstairs and was gone but a moment.

"Everything is there," he said. "I'll just leave it."

"You'll come home with me now, Sales, won't you?" Tod said. "You don't want to stay here all alone, do you?"

"Well—" Sales coughed again. "I'll walk home with you if you want me to, Tod. But I'd rather come back here to sleep."

"Oh, I wouldn't let you walk home with me unless you stayed," Tod said. "Sales, you've done so much for us. You've helped Dad and—" Tod's eyes suddenly stung and he wondered if he could have gotten something in them. "Will you be all right here?"

For some moments Tod had been conscious of street noises that seemed to grow louder. Sales opened the door and a crescendo of happy talk and shouts came to them. Sales grinned.

"They know it now—that the fire has been stopped," Sales said.

The street with its waiting people had come to life. Triumphant yells rose from the crowd as women sped from one group to another. The men talked excitedly and slapped each other on the back. Even the old folks were smiling, and the children raced and played.

"Vincenzo!" An old lady with a shawl over her head ran up to them as Sales and Tod left the house. She poured out a stream of Italian that Tod could not understand.

Sales laughed and answered her in the same language. Then Sales tried to introduce Tod to her, saying that she was their next-door neighbor. But the Italian and the English became so mixed up that finally the three of them were laughing, none too sure of what was being said in either language, but very certain that everything was all right—for wasn't the fire over?

"And she says," Sales explained to Tod, "that all the people around here have promised St. Anthony of Padua that they will celebrate his feast day every year, in thankfulness for their homes being spared, in answer to their prayers to him during the Fire."*

Other people came up to Sales, all speaking Italian. When Tod saw that Sales was among friends, he thought it was time for him to start home.

At that moment, one of the hurdy-gurdies down the street began grinding out a song, "In the Good Old Summer Time." A few people began to sing and

---

* A festive procession is still held each year in Baltimore's Little Italy, on the Sunday closest to June 13, the Feast Day of St. Anthony.

some began to dance. A blast of music came from another grind organ in front of Sales' home. This one, however, was playing "There'll be a Hot Time in the Old Town Tonight."

Everyone on the street had suddenly begun to sing and dance, and the music from one hurdy-gurdy would drown out the music from another. Men and women caught up partners and danced on the brick sidewalks. Even the old people were circling and tapping their feet. Children chased each other around the dancing couples. A hysterical ecstasy seemed to overcome everyone at the good news that the fire was over.

The monkeys, dressed in their red jackets and caps, began to jump up and down, and then, thinking that the size of the crowd called for their usual tricks, they began to make the rounds. Taking off their caps, they held them out, begging for pennies. But since almost every organ grinder had his own monkey, it was soon noticed that monkeys were begging from owners of other monkeys. The men guffawed, then howled with laughter as a monkey would go a-begging to nearby families gathered around their own hurdy-gurdy and their own monkey.

Everything was wonderful, because wasn't the fire over?

Tod, anxious to get started home, tried to talk to Sales alone, but everyone on the street seemed to be greeting Sales. Sales now had a little color in his face, and was talking and laughing in spite of his cold, his wet feet and his sooty clothes.

"Sales," Tod said, "I'll have to go, but are you all right? Maybe you should go to bed."

The Italian woman poured out a stream of words to Sales, nodding toward Tod as she did so.

"She understands English, but she cannot speak it," Sales explained. "She says to tell you, Tod, that she will look after me! As if I needed looking after!" Sales made a face. "She says she will rub goose grease on my chest. Ugh!" He listened as the Italian woman talked.

"Oh! That's better! She says we dance because I am her youngest friend."

Both boys laughed. Tod said "goodbye" and before he could say more, the Italian woman had grabbed Sales and danced off with him. Sales did not look sick anymore. He did not even look tired. He waved "goodbye" and shouted something as he danced away. Tod thought that he said he would help hunt for Gerry, tomorrow.

Tod walked north and he did not feel nearly so tired. Maybe it was because the tunes from the hurdy-gurdies followed him for several blocks. He found himself keeping step to the music of "You Don't Belong to the Regulars, You're only a Volunteer," and sang the words.

You don't belong to the regulars
You're only a volunteer.

You don't belong to the rank and file
But someone holds you dear.
Many a mother's heart will break
But in the coming year
Uncle Sam will take off his hat
To you, Mister Volunteer.

He turned west as soon as he was sure he would
avoid the fire district. As he walked, he looked up
and down every street and alley hoping he might
see Gerry. Of course Debbie had said she would
search for him, but he did not have much hope that
she would find him.

He was so tired that he stumbled. As he pulled
himself to his feet, he saw a crowd of people more
than a block away. A boy about his own age passed
him, going toward the crowd and dragging a younger
boy by the hand.

"Hurry up!" the bigger boy said. "You've just
got to see him. The dog is as big as a pony."

As big as a pony! A dog! Tod was alert immediately. Could Gerry be mixed up in that crowd
somewhere? He saw a policeman detach himself
from the crowd and pull hard on the rope. Tod
gasped. He was sure that Gerry was at the other end
of that rope. That was just the way that Gerry would
act. Even though he couldn't see him, Tod knew that
if his dog did not want to move, no amount of pulling or tugging would budge him, not even the efforts
of a policeman.

184

Policeman! Tod groaned. Gerry was not wearing his new dog tag, so it might go hard with him. But his father had remembered to get it, and it was now safe in his pocket. He pulled it out and put it in his other pocket all alone, so he could get it easily.

He ran toward the crowd, even though he was so tired he could barely move. He must get to Gerry —no one, not the policeman, not anybody on earth could keep him from his dog.

He elbowed his way through the crowd, paying no attention to the policeman or to anyone else. Yes, there lay a heap of brown and black and white fur, with doleful eyes and droopy ears and a wavy tail that didn't show because Gerry had it curled under him, as he mournfully resisted the tugging rope.

"Gerry! My Gerry!" Tod whispered.

The dog came to his feet, making little joyful sounds as Tod took the dog's big head in his arms. Then Gerry barked, just one bark, short and happy. The crowd fell back and the policeman dropped the rope. Neither the crowd or the policeman noticed that Gerry was wagging everything he had, not just his tail, but everything from his middle on back.

Tod held Gerry close to him. Then looking over the dog's head, he wondered if he was seeing things, for there was Debbie, and there was Ham, and the rope tied to Gerry's collar looked very much like Ham's lasso, that Tod had put in his cellar.

The crowd closed around him, and Debbie and Ham started to explain, and Gerry decided to stand on his hind legs and put both paws on Tod's shoulders in happy reunion, as he purred joyfully in Tod's ear. Tod wondered how on earth Gerry had been found. The policeman's voice cut through his thoughts.

"That dog! He'll kill somebody!" the policeman said.

"Oh, no, Gerry wouldn't kill anybody!" Tod assured the policeman, who towered above him, very big and very stern.

"Bite somebody! That's what he will do," the policeman said.

"Gerry doesn't bite!" Tod said, patiently and politely.

"He doesn't have to bite!" For some reason the policeman was yelling. "That dog is so big, he'll scare a person to death! Besides, where's his new license? He doesn't have any." He picked up the rope to lead Gerry away.

How lucky that his father had given him the license. It was a good thing that he had it ready, too. He took it from his pocket and proudly he showed it to the policeman, and started to explain.

"You see, sir, the fire—" Tod began.

"Oh, yes, *the fire*—" Somehow the words had changed the policeman entirely. He even smiled sympathetically and said, "I understand."

Tod was to find that the magic words, *the fire*, excused anything and everything for many weeks to come in the city of Baltimore.

"Get the dog home," the policeman said, but in a very kindly voice.

Debbie and Ham had kept quiet, but now Ham grabbed the rope and spoke up.

"Sure. Sure. Gerry will go with us, Tod, now that you are here. That was why he wouldn't move. But he likes me, Tod, he *does*." Ham seemed very anxious to prove this. He pulled at the rope, but nothing happened. Gerry sat back on his haunches.

"It's been like that all afternoon," Debbie said. "We found him near Mike's house. Ham had gotten his lasso from Cora, and when Gerry went so fast, we were afraid he would get away, so Ham tied the lasso to his collar, and Gerry sat down and he's been there ever since."

"Come on, Gerry." Tod took hold of the rope with Ham and they both started to pull.

The dog sat. He looked at Tod with big sad eyes.

"You see," the policeman said. "That's what he does. He just sits. You've got to get that dog off the streets—license or no license—or else I'll have to turn him over to the Society for the Prevention of Cruelty to Animals."

Now Tod was really alarmed, for Gerry had never refused to go anywhere with him. He took the dog's big head in his arms.

"What's wrong? Gerry, boy, you have to come home. Home, Gerry," and Tod pulled on the rope.

The dog pricked up his ears. He looked intelligent, but he wouldn't move.

187

"I got my lasso from Cora just so I could take Gerry home when we found him," Ham complained. "It was good I had it, because Gerry was running so fast we couldn't keep up with him."

"Ham," Tod asked, "Was he running *toward* home?"

"Well, yes, he was," Ham said grudgingly.

So Gerry had been going in the direction of home! In that case there was no reason for a leash on Gerry. He'd never had a leash. So with complete disregard for the policeman, and the crowd, Tod untied the lasso and left the dog free.

"No, no! Don't let him loose!" people shouted to the policeman. The crowd shrank from the dog and no one seemed to want to be in the front row nearest him. The policeman said nothing, but gripped his nightstick.

Tod looped the lasso and handed it to Ham. "Take it where Gerry can't see it," Tod said and Ham took the rope and hid it behind his back.

"Come on, Gerry," Tod said quietly. The dog rose, and followed Tod, walking calmly at Tod's side where Tod could touch his head.

The people in the crowd started to laugh, and someone said "Hurrah!"

"Thank goodness!" the policeman said, as he took off his helmet and wiped his forehead.

The three children and the dog walked toward home, in the gathering twilight, and Debbie and Ham tried to explain how they had found Gerry.

"We hunted all around our neighborhood this morning," Debbie said, "and nobody had seen him. Then I thought I would try at Mike's house, but before we got there we saw Gerry trotting along all by himself."

"And me, me too, I helped, didn't I, Debbie, didn't I?" Ham said. "I got my lasso and went with you this morning and this afternoon too, didn't I?"

"Oh yes. Ham helped. He certainly did. But Tod, I wanted to have Gerry home by the time you got there." Debbie sounded disappointed, and Tod remembered that she had wanted to prove that girls were smarter than boys.

Tod was so glad to have his dog back that he was almost willing to say that girls *were* smarter than boys. He grinned at Debbie and pushed her shoulder.

"You did find him, though, Debbie, even if you couldn't get him home," he said.

"Yes, I did, didn't I?" Debbie smiled, and it was like the sun coming out on a cloudy day. Her face brightened and her blue eyes shone, as she wrinkled her nose like a bunny rabbit and began to skip.

"And I helped," Ham said. "I was the one who said we'd take the lasso so we could lead him home, wasn't I, Debbie?" Ham moved in front of Tod so he could talk directly into Tod's face.

For some reason, Ham no longer looked mean and he didn't squint in that silly way that he thought was like a cowboy, and he seemed very earnest and anxious for Gerry to like him. Then, as Ham walked

189

backwards trying to talk to Tod, he forgot to hide the lasso, and the coiled rope grazed Gerry's nose. Gerry sat down. They stopped, all three of them.

Tod turned to Ham.

"Ham, you'll just have to go home alone, or else get rid of that lasso. Gerry doesn't like it."

"But he likes me, Tod, he *does!*" Ham threw his arms around Gerry's neck, but the lasso again touched Gerry and the dog pulled away from him.

Ham's whole face sagged. His mouth turned down and for a moment Tod thought he was going to cry, but he squared his shoulders and walked away from them without a word, going back the way they had come.

Gerry arose like the most obedient dog in the whole wide world and followed Tod and Debbie.

They had gone almost a block when Ham came running and caught up with them. Tod saw he no longer held the lasso.

"Threw the lasso in the ash can," Ham said. He fondled Gerry's head and talked to the big dog, and Gerry rewarded him by snuggling close and wagging his tail madly.

Then they were once more on their way home.

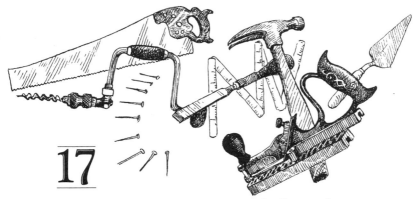

17

The next morning Gerry padded up the stairs and woke Tod with one lick of his tongue. Tod was blissfully happy. Gerry lay down, stretching his full length, his wagging tail thumping the floor as he watched Tod dress.

Tod's high spirits faded, however, as he remembered what his father had been through. He thought of him standing in the factory, his face smudged with dirt, his shirt with a hole in it, and his hat with the crown burned out.

Yesterday evening when he and Gerry had arrived home, he had found his father and Betty Ann already there, brought home by Dr. Waid in his own carriage. The doctor had given Mr. Morton a sedative and put him to bed.

Betty Ann seemed none the worse for her experience. When Tod came home she hugged him and called him "brother," and she hugged Gerry, too.

This morning, Tod dug into his clothes closet for his last pair of shoes. They were scuffed and worn, but now they were all he possessed. The two pairs he had worn on Sunday and Monday would never be wearable again.

He would have to buy shoes just as all the other boys did. He had never worn anything but The Morton Shoe. Of course he knew they were *good shoes*, but he had always wanted to try some others. He'd like to buy some at one of the big department stores, like Hutzler's or Hochschild Kohn.

He dressed quickly and soon he was ready to go to breakfast. At the head of the back stairs he could hear his mother and Cora deep in argument.

"But Mrs. Morton," Cora said, "let me take a cup of coffee to Mr. Morton so he can sip it in bed before he gets up. He can face the world better after he has a cup of coffee."

"No, Cora," his mother said firmly, "Mr. Morton doesn't like his coffee in bed. He'd think the world had come to an end. If he isn't down soon, I'll go up and see how he is feeling."

Tod had heard his father moving around. As he went down the back stairs, he heard his father going down the front stairs, and they both arrived in the dining room about the same time.

"Good morning!" his father said, just as he did every morning. Yet today was not the same as other mornings.

Cora stationed herself in back of Mr. Morton's chair, trying to get him to eat, but he ate little. Nor did he seem to want to talk, nor to tell about what he had been through.

It was Gerry, finally, who made his father talk. Gerry, in his accustomed place under the table, let out a deep, contented sigh, so loud that it sounded like the snorting of a horse. Everybody laughed, even his father.

"You found Gerry all right, didn't you? What happened? Did he come home by himself?" Mr. Morton asked.

Tod tried to tell him how Gerry had been lost twice. It sounded awfully crazy, and Tod realized that it really *was*, and he wasn't surprised when his father looked puzzled as he got deeper into the search for Gerry. Then Betty Ann's face got sort of pink, and when she coughed and looked at him knowingly, he knew Mike must have told her why he had locked Gerry in his yard.

He was glad of the interruption at that moment —a familiar "thump" that meant the Sunpaper was being delivered. He ran to the door and his father followed him. Charles, the newsboy, was waiting for them.

"It's even more special, today, your Sunpaper," Charles said. "You should be awful glad I'm your friend, Tod. These Sunpapers are scarce."

"You're a good boy, Charles," Mr. Morton said. "I know from what we all went through yesterday that we are lucky to have our Sunpaper. Here is a little gift for you," and his father gave Charles a whole *fifty cents*, and Charles thanked him all the way down the front steps.

His father brought the Sunpaper into the dining room, and everyone clustered around him. This morning there were no rules about not reading over anyone's shoulder. Everyone read the paper at the same time.

"You see," Cora said. She was standing in back of all of them, reading as fast as anyone. "You see, there wasn't one life lost, not one." Cora was content.

"It says that the part that was destroyed was the original town of Baltimore, almost exactly as it was laid out in 1729 and 1730," Betty Ann read.

The Sunpaper was smudged in spots and some of it could not be read at all. Tod pointed out that one page said, *"The Sun,* Baltimore, Tuesday Morning, Tuesday," and chuckled to see that newspapers made mistakes too. His father was quick to reprimand him.

"They got the paper out, son. They managed, somehow. They were burned out and they had to go to Washington to publish the paper, but this morning, in spite of everything, we have our paper."

Tod felt very small for having laughed at a little mistake like the repeating of a word in a headline when the Sun Building itself had been burned out.

"But Todhunter," Mrs. Morton had withheld her questions, but now that her husband was talking freely she could no longer hold back her curiosity. "Do they know how it started? How on earth could a fire make so much headway so quickly?"

"They are not sure, but the talk at the moment is that the wind carried a lighted match, or a cigarette, or a cigar through the grating on the sidewalk of John E. Hurst's. They think it lay there and smoldered among the blankets and the cotton goods stored there, perhaps it lay there all night, but it didn't flare into open flame until Sunday morning."

And the whole heart of Baltimore burned because of that, Tod thought.

Mr. Morton was leafing through the pages of the paper and talking at the same time.

"The paper says that 1500 buildings have been burned, and 140 acres devastated," Mr. Morton said. He reached the editorial page and read aloud—

"It is the duty of every Baltimorean . . . to devote his energies to the task of making Baltimore a greater city. . . ."

Turning the pages again he went back to the front page and read the big advertisement, and he sat up straight and took a deep breath.

"Look!" he said, pointing to the front page.

Flamboyantly, boastfully, a half-page advertisement said, "George A. Fuller Co. Building Contractor."

A smile touched his father's face. "We're not licked, we Baltimoreans, we're just burned out. A good ad, that of George Fuller. I must tell him so. You know what it says, son? It says more, much more than the printed word. It says 'Arise and build.' I'm going downtown." He rose from the table.

"Oh, take me, Dad," Betty Ann begged. "Please, Dad."

"Certainly I'll take you." Her father looked at her fondly. "Women will have to help with this job—yes, and children, too. Come on, Tod."

In a few minutes the three of them were ready.

"Take care of yourself, Todhunter, dear," his mother said, patting his father on the back. "Don't do too much. Everything will come out all right."

"Sure, Lizzie, sure." His father realized he had used his mother's old name, and his father and mother looked at each other for a moment, and they laughed and laughed. But there wasn't anything funny, so why were they laughing?

Tod gave Gerry an extra pat on the nose as they left the house. As soon as they came out the door, the sharp odor of smoke came to them, but it was a dead smell, not like that of living clouds of smoke. Streetcars were running, but not very often, and not very far. They took the Carey Street car on Carrollton Avenue, but it seemed they had no sooner gotten on before the conductor said, "Far as we go." They found themselves on Fayette Street, but quite a distance from the center of the city.

"Look, Dad," Betty Ann said. "Look at that black smoke. Maybe the fire isn't out yet."

"Lady, it's out," said a strange man. "It will smolder for a long time, though." And he walked on. Betty Ann looked startled, but they were to find that today, total strangers talked to each other, and news and rumors flew from person to person.

The militia was in complete charge of the burned-out area. A soldier told them they must get a pass at the Court House if they needed to enter, but that women were not allowed at all.

"In that case," Mr. Morton said, "you can both see some of the devastation, and then go home. I'll get a pass because I must try to find out where the insurance people are, and I will try to get into the Savings Bank of Baltimore, but I'll walk a block or so with you."

Tod looked at Betty Ann and she grinned, and they both understood perfectly well where they would go when Mr. Morton left them. Where else but the Western Union?

Together, they walked as far as Baltimore Street, and looked toward Jones' Falls. There was nothing left. Here and there a corner of a building stuck up into the air for three or four stories—just a corner—nothing more. A few gutted buildings, weird skeletons, could be seen through—all the way through to the other side. Mostly it was rubble and rubbish that still smoked with dying flames. Tod made out the Equitable Building, the framework still standing—but just a shell.

"Go down to Pratt Street. You just go and look," a strange man said to them.

They started toward Pratt Street. Tod noticed

a restlessness that seemed to possess everyone. People walked and seemed unable to stand still. They seemed to have something of great importance to do, but nobody did anything. There was nothing to do.

Over and over, Tod heard the words spoken grandly, ". . . clear the ruins, and start rebuilding." Clear the ruins? They were too hot to touch. Start rebuilding? How could they while the rubble still smoldered?

They came to Pratt Street. Rubble, ruin, and devastation were all they could see. They walked eastward.

Then they saw it—a building at Pratt and Light Streets! Festooned with ice, draped like a bride in white sequins that sparkled in the morning light, Tod saw a bulding completely sheathed in ice and icicles.

"They saved it!" a man said. "The Anderson and Ireland Building! You know it is a hardware store, but the building was full of gunpowder and bullets and ammunition of all kinds because they sell a lot of hunting equipment. The firemen were afraid if the building ever caught fire it would automatically shoot up the town. So six hoses played on it all day yesterday. They drew the water from the harbor there."

Tod saw that men came and talked to his father. Some of them Tod knew but others he had never seen before. They all talked very loudly and waved their arms around.

"... and widen Charles Street. Make Light Street wider, too," one man said. "And rebuild the wharves."

Tod looked at Light Street. He glanced toward Charles Street. Bricks, mortar, all sorts of odds and ends of masonry had fallen all over the two streets, so that at the moment there wasn't so much as a foot-path to be seen.

A workman near Tod looked at his new gloves. "They tell us we are to start work immediately," he said, "but those hot bricks would burn the gloves off of me. I bought these in a little shop over in East Baltimore. They were the last pair they had. Do you know they say there aren't enough gloves in the whole city to put on the workmen when they commence to clear the ruins? And all the manufacturers have been burned out completely."

"We'll furnish the gloves," Betty Ann spoke to this perfect stranger. "I'll get some of the church women on the job. We'll knit them, and we'll see that they have gloves."

Tod looked at Betty Ann in astonishment, not because she had spoken to the strange man, but because she had offered to knit gloves. Betty Ann's knitting was so terrible that no poor workman should have to go through the hardship of wearing anything *she* had knit.

"You can't knit, Sis." Tod grinned. "You know you can't."

"No, but I can get the women together, and *they*

can knit. Some of the women at the church are very good knitters. I'll beg the wool—and the women would love to do it."

Tod looked at Betty Ann with a new respect. His sister was smart. It was true she could not knit, but she was trying to do the thing that she knew how to do—get together the women who could knit— organizing, Betty Ann called it.

Tod saw a commotion, a big reception of someone by the men around his father, and his father was hugging someone, and looking pleased as he could be. Tod and Betty Ann watched and wondered, and then they saw it was Mr. Uvaldi. His father had always said "Mr. Uvaldi is all right," and he guessed that they had all better forget the rest of it. If Mr. Uvaldi was going to buy shoes from the new Morton Shoe Factory, his shoes would be all right, too.

His father came over to him and Betty Ann. "Mr. Uvaldi has found out where the insurance adjusters are. Seems they are all at the Royal Arcanum Building opposite the Hotel Rennert. So I'll go along with him. You two children can find your way home alone."

"Yes, Dad," Betty Ann said, "but we'll stop at the Western Union first, to see Mike."

"Oh, yes. Well, that's outside the fire district, but you'll have to go all the way around to the north to get there."

"We know," Tod laughed.

They left Mr. Morton and started once more,

going around to the north—just as they had done yesterday—just as they had done on Sunday. Sunday —it seemed years ago, because so much had happened.

Passing Lexington Market, Tod finally got up enough courage to say to Betty Ann, "Do you think I could ask Mike if there are any messages that I could deliver, *today*? It's awful to have to wait until next summer."

"Sure, Tod, go ahead." Betty Ann said. "Lots of good things may come out of this fire, as well as bad things. Dad says maybe he'll let me work with him, maybe as cashier or something. I could even answer the telephone, if Dad puts one in."

Betty Ann could do that, Tod thought, without offending the shoemakers. They were a very independent group and they might not like working side by side with the daughter of the boss; but if she were the cashier, maybe they would accept her. He didn't even want to think about the despised telephone, although one might very well be installed in the new Morton Shoe Company.

"But Betty Ann, don't you want to be a teacher?"

"Oh, yes, but not if I can have some kind of a job with shoes. I'll finish my training course, but Brother, you know how I love shoes!"

Yes, she did, and her face brightened up when she talked about *shoes*. She was looking mighty happy today, a kind of shiny happy, so much so that it showed.

"Even if I married Mike, I could do that," she said.

There it was. Somehow he'd known it all along, but he had hoped it would not happen, because then Mike would no longer be *his* friend.

"Then Mike would be your brother-in-law," Betty Ann said dreamily. "That's next best to being your brother."

But of course! He had never thought of it that way. Mike would be *family*!

After that it didn't seem long before they were at the House of Welsh, and were climbing the stairs to the Western Union.

Mike was there in the office. He jumped up, leaving his key open. Quickly he motioned to a man to come and take his wire for him.

He came toward them, pushing back his heavy hair as he came. His eyes sort of sparkled. He said "Hello!" to Tod but Tod thought he might just as well not be there, because Mike acted like there was nobody in the room except Betty Ann. It wasn't as if Mike and Betty Ann had anything important to say to each other. They said ordinary things like "How are you?" But they looked at each other, and when they didn't say anything there seemed to be an awful lot that they weren't saying.

Tod was disgusted. He didn't think Mike was acting like a "brother." How was he ever going to break in and ask Mike about delivering messages?

Finally, however, Mike turned to him.

"Tod, maybe you'd like to work for a few days.

Governor Warfield called the legislature together last night, and they declared a legal holiday for a whole week, from February 8 to February 15. You won't have to go to school, so maybe you'd like to deliver some messages."

Tod held his breath, and then let it out all at once. He thought he said, "Yes, thank you," but afterward he was never really sure. Mike took him over to the Superintendent of Messengers.

"Oh, Tod," the Superintendent said, "you are the one that delivered that message out on the Harford Road, aren't you? Maybe you'd like to work a few days—just during the emergency."

"Oh, yes, yes, sir, I could do it," Tod said.

"All right. I'll put you on the payroll. It's Tod Morton, isn't it? Here are three messages. They're all in the same direction and not too far away. Think you could manage them?"

"Oh, yes, sir," Tod said. He asked Betty Ann to explain to his mother and he started for the door.

"Wait a minute, Tod!" the Superintendent called him back. "Here's a cap for you. We like the boys to wear the cap if possible."

The cap. The cap that said "The Western Union Telegraph Company." He put it on carefully and stuffed his own cap in his pocket.

He went toward the door, walking with great dignity, stiff and straight. He must live up to the cap. He went down the stairs and once outside, he could see his reflection in the window. He tilted his cap over his left eye. Then he pulled it down over his *right* eye, but neither way made him look like a *serious* Western Union messenger boy. Finally he set it straight on his head, and frowned. It was just right, particularly if he frowned *hard*.

He started walking.

Let his father and Mr. Uvaldi build the shoe stores and factories, yes and Betty Ann, too.

As for him, he would work for Western Union, like Mike. Today he was a messenger boy, but later on he would be a real Morse operator, and he would talk to the whole world. For the Western Union would find new ways to send messages across continents, over oceans, around the world.

He looked toward the Equitable Building. Gutted and skeleton-like, it was still standing. Maybe it could be rebuilt!

He stopped and laughed out loud at himself, just as he had laughed at those other Baltimoreans this morning. In the streets of this ruined city they were all dreaming of a new city—a Bigger and Better Baltimore.

He patted the messages in his pocket. He was doing his duty like the Sunpaper said, and he smiled as he wondered if duty could be a happy thing.

He set his cap a little more firmly on his head. He tried hard to frown, but couldn't quite make it as he started to whistle "I Can't Tell Why I Love You, But I Do," and went on his way to deliver his messages.

Designed by Victor A. Curran

Composed in Linotype Caledonia,
with Goudy Handtooled and Chisel display,
by the Maryland Linotype Composition Company,
Baltimore, Maryland

Jacket and cover color separation by Capper, Inc.,
Knoxville, Tennessee

Jacket and cover printed by Rugby Associates, Inc.,
Knoxville, Tennessee

Book printed on 60-pound Glatfelter Offset,
hardbound in Holliston Sturdetan and bound in paper
by Fairfield Graphics, Fairfield, Pennsylvania